Praise for Stephen Graham Jones and *The Least of My Scars*

"A grim, funny, stylish hallucination of a book—murderous insanity seen from the inside out. You'll be revolted by this guy, but he'll fascinate you too." —Jack Ketchum

"*The Least of My Scars* shows how a serial killer's paradise and a serial killer's hell are really the same place. A dark and steady noir which pulls the rug painfully out from under your feet at the end." —Brian Evenson

"[Jones's] writing is hallucinogenic, varied, fascinating. . . . Big names in writing [come] to mind: Pynchon, David Foster Wallace, even Faulkner." —*New Pages*

"The constant threat or fact of violence in [his] stories combined with Jones's idiosyncratic, staccato prose makes for gripping and visceral reading." —*Publishers Weekly* on *Bleed into Me*

"Jones has done in prose what you sometimes see in engineering drawings where a complex piece of machinery is 'exploded,' with each component set apart from the others so that every aspect may be studied closely."
—*Austin Chronicle* on *The Fast Red Road: A Plainsong*

"My hat is off to Stephen Graham Jones, because he is the kind of author that makes the frustrated writer inside every book reviewer cringe with self-doubt." —*Popmatters*

THE LEAST OF MY SCARS

THE LEAST OF MY SCARS

STEPHEN GRAHAM JONES

INTEGRATED MEDIA
NEW YORK

An excerpt from *The Least of My Scars* first appeared in *Plots With Guns*

ISBN: 978-1-5040-9949-3

This edition published in 2025 by Open Road Integrated Media, Inc.
180 Maiden Lane
New York, NY 10038
www.openroadmedia.com

for Guy Intoci, for all the saves

and for Chick Chambers

THE LEAST OF MY SCARS

no creature can learn that which his heart has no shape to hold

—Cormac McCarthy

So I'm sitting there in the slant of light from the afternoon sun when there's this knock on my door.

"You order pizza?" I mumble in the general direction of the kitchen, just a countertop away, but I'm the only one here.

For now.

I laugh and cover it with my hand, like there's a peephole mounted backwards, me in its sights.

Spend enough time alone with yourself, you might start pretending, too.

"Too late for the mail . . ." I go on, tapping the butt of the remote into the fabric of my recliner, lifting my wrist and angling it over to cut the glare and study my watch.

Six on the nose.

"Somebody sending me flowers?" I say out loud then, just part of the routine. "Got a secret admirer there?"

I can't help smiling.

Another knock, more timid this time.

I ratchet the footrest down loud enough to be heard then haul myself up from the chair. Walk to the window instead of the door.

Across the way there's televisions flickering through windows, there's dinners getting reheated, there's women curled around a secret they'll never tell and there's men staring at a little place on the wall like it maybe just spoke to them.

I draw the drapes on them all.

"Hold on," I call across the room.

Maybe I'm getting dressed, or hiding the weed, or finishing a phone call. Putting on my man mask.

On the way to the door I'm sure to touch five things, each above waist level, for luck. The reason they have to be above waist level is that makes me bend my arm a bit, expend the effort. Just dragging the pad of your finger over whatever's in your way's asking for disaster.

Lampshade, piping on the couch, tabletop, whorl in the paint on the wall, and empty picture frame.

I'm ready.

"Who is it?" I singsong into the back side of the door, one hand to the knob, the other pinching the chain.

What I'm waiting for here's what I'm always waiting for: somebody to complete the joke. Just anything—"Orange, Orange-who?"

Nobody ever tries, though.

"Guess this is no joke, then," I say, hiding it with the chain scraping back.

But there's always the chance they've heard, too.

You've got to have some fun, I mean.

And it's not pizza, and not a package, and not flowers. I look to the left and the right to be sure, then to the guy standing there, just waiting for me to catch his eye so he can be sure to hold it. Likely he read in some magazine about pack hierarchy and prison society, and how if you look away, that's your weakness shining through.

Fucking amateur.

I lower my face some, like I don't want him to remember it.

"You're him?" I say.

He nods, keeps his hands in the pockets of his sweat jacket. Walking through the dried-up lobby downstairs, his hood was over his head, I know. His hair's still all messed up. There's no cameras down there, though, and everybody else has their own rats to be killing, their own fires to stomp out.

But when you're doing something, something you maybe don't want on a marquee so much, sure, the whole world's watching you, right?

I know, I've been there.

For thirty-four years to be precise.

Looking over my shoulder even in the broad daylight. Unmentionable stuff crusted around my fingernails.

That was the old me, though.

These are the new days, the good days.

I swallow what wants to be a smile here, step aside for Mr. Hoodie.

He ducks through, past, giving me some berth but being real casual about it. Casing the joint, as he might say it.

What you see is what you get, pretty much: an entryway dining room, a living room that spills over sideways into a kitchenette, one door on the opposite wall opening onto a bathroom and another onto a hall. My bedroom's down there, and then the other room, all the way back. Beside us, right behind Hoodie, the tall narrow door of the vacuum cleaner closet. My winter jacket's in there too, I suppose. Probably out of fashion by now.

Hoodie pretends not to, but he holds his breath, listening to me not lock the door.

"This going to take long?" he asks, fidgety now, hooking his chin down to the street.

"Your ride?" I say, still thinking about the vacuum cleaner, then finally nodding to myself about it.

On cue Hoodie threads a cigarette out from his mop of hair, pops his eyes up for permission.

"Not my place," I shrug, and cross to the kitchen, ferret a soup can up from the trash for him to ash into.

We're both just scrubs here is what I'm telling him. Cogs in the great machinery of this bad old city.

"Should I tell her thirty?" he says, cocking his cell open with one hand, his eyes narrow from his own smoke.

"Twenty," I say back, and he nods, considers, then's on my side enough to slap the cell phone shut, spin it into his pocket. *Kid* Hoodie, maybe. That's his name.

"So he just said. . . ?" he leads off.

I nod, reach up to a top cabinet but do it slow too, all my hands in view the whole time, like he's got a gun. And he may.

It's just a board game, though.

He laughs about it.

"Trouble?" he says, exhaling to the side.

I toss it down on the table so it'll be sure to rattle like it's supposed to.

Yeah, Trouble. That popper in the middle, the little holes for your piece to jump in, the whole bit.

I used to play it with my brother, growing up. Not this exact game, but one enough like it. Marathons we had. This and Risk. But Risk takes too long. Not that I haven't done it before. You get lonely, I mean. Hungry for company.

Anyway.

Kid Hoodie sits down at the table being real gentle with everything, like this is a dream he can rip through on accident.

"I'm just supposed to play you?" he asks, tapping into the soup can now, thank you.

"He didn't tell you?"

He shrugs, pulls his lower lip into his mouth and rolls it between his teeth a bit.

"Just this," he says, opening his fingers to the apartment all around us. "Four thirty-nine Chessire Arms."

"*Four* thirty-nine?" I say, careful to get the numbers right—they change—"that's up on the fourth floor, man. Where do you think you are?"

His face drops, his eyes narrow, but before he can start breathing fast or anything I laugh through my nose, push his blue game pieces over to him.

"Real fucking funny," he says, ashing harder now, tough guy.

I keep laughing, can't help it.

What he thinks he's here for, I don't really know. Maybe I'm supposed to be passing on a professional evaluation of sorts on him: Yes, he exhibits control, patience, and diligence, would make a fine hood, thug, or lackey, at least as far as playing Trouble with him would indicate. Or maybe it's different: he's a witness for the prosecution, one with his hand not out, so much, but not all the way in either; he's somebody's bad-luck ex and I'm supposed to arbitrate a child support repayment scheme; his brother's an assistant horse trainer, can fix a race if he, say, had to. Or he's a narc, a rival, a cable guy who was late one too many times, and on and on.

It doesn't matter.

What does is that, earlier today he was standing in some pool hall or bar, some bank lobby or motel room, and some nobody, some guy with bloodshot eyes, some girl with an unbreakable heart, handed over a folded little piece of paper, one they knew better than to look at.

Scrawled on it in pencil, my address. Just that.

Now this.

The popper goes down and comes back up fast, the rounded-corner dice insane with anger, buzzing like a pair of wasps under my cupped palm. But they give up their number. You would, too.

Kid Hoodie laughs at it, at them, at all of this.

He's into the game, on the edge of his seat, sucking on his cigarette like it's a straw to his only air.

He makes the first corner, pushes the popper down and closes his lips in silent prayer.

"You've done this before," I tell him, my last yellow piece still close to home, and his eyes glitter a *hell yes* back to me.

"What if I win?" he says, his right knee a jackhammer with nothing to do.

In answer, I tilt my head just enough to the high vent in the wall over my shoulder.

His knee goes still, and he stabs his mouth with the cigarette again.

"It's not so much about that," I say, my voice so fake, so level.

He gets it, goes robot too, manages to look at the vent in the most obvious way possible every ten seconds: by looking at everything *but* it.

And so we play, and I get up once for two beers, and somewhere in there I ask him where he grew up.

He comes even more awake, understands that we're getting to the meat of the thing here. That the game's just a diversion, an excuse to be sitting at a table. That I'm feeling him out.

"Duluth," he spits.

I pop the dice.

"You?" he says back.

It's only polite.

I lift a vague shoulder, study the closed window, and tell him just over the river. That I remember being a kid and my best friend's mom crying from when the ferry went down, because she thought she'd known somebody on it. Everything turned out all right, though. At least until her son got to be about sixteen.

He nods like this ferry exists, sure, everybody knows that, and pops the dice.

They rattle, roll, stop.

He moves one short of what they add up to and I correct him, even though it's not to my advantage. At least game-wise. Okay: Trouble-wise. Because of course this is all a game. The best kind.

"So you like it?" he says, since we're best friends and all now.

"What?"

"You know . . . this."

"This?"

"I mean—"

I stare at him until it becomes obvious that that's precisely what I'm doing. "What do you think we're doing here?" I say, almost at a whisper now. "Is this a drug deal? There any money on the table? Have you ordered a hit from me using some Morse eyebrow code, or is that what you were tapping out with your heel there?"

He's backpedaling now, in his head. Falling all over himself.

I hold my hand up, palm out, then lower it slowly to the popper, let it explode again.

"I just consult," I say. "Time to time. Special interest stuff, know what I mean?"

He does, he does. Is the only one who does.

There's no girlfriend down in the car, either. There's no parking like that for four blocks, almost. This apartment is no accident.

"However," I tell him, moving my yellow piece four spaces, touching down on all the holes on the way, the last twice, "and this is strictly"—the vent, Kid Hoodie, the vent—"Are you a cop? Yes or no."

He shakes his head no, then says it out loud, even musters the proper amount of insult.

I nod like I already knew this, but had to ask.

And so we play on, each rounding the corner onto our home stretches, him trying desperately to lose but you can't control that damn popper. That's the beauty of it.

The pieces, though, yeah. They're not in any hard plastic shell.

What I do with my lead one is take it by the yellow knob at top, go to move it the two spaces I've rolled but drop it on the second hop, so it clatters off the plastic rim of the board, is skittering for the edge of the table.

Kid Hoodie, being the fast draw specialist he is, nabs it at the last moment, then holds it there above all that open space, pinched like a stubby little joint.

However.

The sleeve of his sweatshirt is bloated, thick, clumsy.

It brushes his soup can just enough to dislodge it.

I do the rest. In trying to catch it—my part of this rescue effort, since he's already saving the game—my thigh bangs up into the table.

It's all just split-second, too. Real photo-finish stuff.

I've had so much time to practice, though. To go through it all in my head, every which way. Sometimes I can't even go to sleep from thinking so much. Or from remembering, doing it over and over again, better each time. The hammering of your heart's a thing that can keep you awake all night if you let it. Especially if it doesn't matter when you wake up, or what you're wearing when you answer the door.

So my leg hits the table, and the soup can, on the same side as the Trouble piece, meaning that hand's occupied, the soup can just gracefully slips off the table.

In his other hand, my speed technician's managed to save his beer, at least.

"Shi-it," I say, wiping my own beer from my pants leg then spreading my fingers away from the stickiness.

Kid Hoodie laughs at all the bad luck in the air this afternoon, takes another drag, reaches down for the spilled soup can.

I lean over, grin some involuntary displeasure at the ash coating the top of the carpet.

"It's no—" he starts, tilting the can over to scoop what he can up, but I stop him.

"It's nothing," I say, standing, my hand on his arm, keeping him from the ash. "I'll just," and I do: the tall narrow closet, the vacuum cleaner. I even hand him the floppy-headed old-fashioned plug, for the socket behind his chair.

"Sorry," he says, then laughs about it, this direction we're going: two grown men, criminal men, worried about a little dingy spot on the carpet.

I nod, my smile fake on the outside but so deep on the inside.

The vacuum cleaner winds up, whines on, coughs out fine, fine dust through the fabric bag.

When the roller won't turn I uncork the hose, and it sucks the ash up like the nothing it is.

I'm not looking right at him either, but still, I can see the question on Kid Hoodie's face. Can read it exactly: *I thought this wasn't your place?*

I love my job.

"Mother of a—" I say, raising the hand I was leaning on, that was just in the carpet. I rub my fingers together like they've got some shit on them now too, and, instead of wiping the shit back—this is my place, after all—I just apply the end of the hose, sticking each finger in one at a time, like how a hand-dryer in a bathroom might work, in some other, better world.

Kid Hoodie narrows his eyes in something like appreciation, something like a shared joke, but then I'm racing my
other hand up the hose, trying to crimp it.

"What?" he says, looking at the vacuum cleaner with new
eyes, I'm pretty sure.

"Unplug it," I tell him, my voice dialed all the way back to
pissed off.

I waggle my fingers to show him they're all there, it's not
that, no teeth in this hose, but then do the wedding-ring rub,
to show him what's missing here.

"I lost some weight this year," I explain, holding the vacuum
up on the chance the ring'll come traipsing down the hose for
me. It doesn't. "She's going to have my ass on a silver platter," I
say, going to my knees now, to unzip the bag.

Kid Hoodie tries not to smile here.

That's good.

Not that it matters.

"Guess I'm going to need a—" I say, finishing by pointing
with my face at the paper towel roll way over on the other side
of the table, and when he turns to reach for it, I push my hand
into the vacuum cleaner bag, find the smooth wooden handle
right where I left it, then stand behind him, the dusty little
twelve-inch hatchet loose in my right hand, wormy little fibers
floating all through the air now like smoke.

The blade isn't as sharp as it should be, but you can make
up for that.

I come down on him like judgment, hard enough that, later
there'll be a shadow of me, a little. Where the mist of blood
didn't spray the wall.

As for Kid Hoodie, the third chop's the one that goes all
the way through to the face. The notched corner of the silver
head pushes out through the always-fragile bone of his right

cheek, plants him smack to the table. Naptime, junior. Nighty night.

I laugh again now, smile for the camera that's not in the vent, and touch five low things on the way to the door, to set the chain. Five low things in thanks, I mean, because that's what you do, and lo to those who would forget.

My name is William Colton Hughes.

You haven't heard of me.

By the third day, Kid Hoodie's stopped entertaining me.

I eat breakfast across from him, and, because we're buds now, reach across, shake some dry cereal into the back of his head. But he likes milk too.

"Hold on, hold on," I grumble, and come back from the kitchen with the jug, tip it in.

It runs out his tear ducts, his nose. Coats his lips on the way down.

I slap him behind the ear, because he should have known better.

The smeary milk—it's not red anymore, but has these black little impurities in it—collects on the table, walls itself up at the edge until the surface tension breaks and it can drip down into the soppy mess the carpet is.

And yeah, some would use plastic here, at least linoleum or tile, but I don't like the way that feels on bare feet at two in the morning, when everything's dark and haunted. And anyway, am I going to doll the place up like it's being remodeled, to keep this big plastic drop cloth from looking out of place? And then just live like that, always trapped in that deadspace after the before picture, but before the after?

No thanks.

As for the carpet, it's not even stretched right, is just hooked onto the tack boards.

You can reuse it a time or two if you don't want to mess with rolling it up, too. All you have to do is keep it sprayed with scotch guard. Saturated, I mean. Layer after layer, like you're trying to paint it clear, fucking erase it.

It wouldn't be good enough for any forensics team with half a degree between them and a lunch hour to kill, but it won't show the stain too much, and the smell, well. If you can't handle the smells, then maybe you should go back in time, have a little heart-to-heart with your guidance counselor.

"Sorry," I say to Kid Hoodie, about slapping him around like that.

Sometimes my temper gets the better of me.

In a plastic baggie on the table is his wallet, his keys, his cute little cell phone, a little music player thing, and the automatic that was supposed to have kept him safe.

So far the cell phone's only rang twice.

Each time I watched it tremble on the table like it was about to unfold its new wet wings, lift itself into the air, ride the waves and signals home.

In the wallet, like you'd expect, are IDs that don't quite match, a clutch of cash stuffed in just any old way, in some stupid order, and a picture of a girl I think must be Sister Hoodie. Either when she was ten or now, I'm not sure. There's no tells in the background either. The living room's Christmased up, and Christmas doesn't belong to any specific decade.

As for the cash, I bake it in the oven, just to see what happens.

At a touch over four hundred degrees, preheated, it takes twelve minutes for the first flame to lick up.

I swirl the black flakes down the drain, leave the sink running.

The mistake so many guys make is that they keep the money, stash it away in some hideyhole, promise themselves to only spend it on coke floats or something, but then never do. Instead they get busted with six thousand in small bills. Six thousand they can't explain, after they've taken care of everything else so well.

And it's not like I have any use for money anymore.

Sunlight though, yeah.

From four-fifteen until six—this is in summers, mind—the sun comes through the window in my living room.

My chair's arranged to catch it.

Used to, pirates all died from scurvy, because there's no vitamin C out on the high seas.

The same thing could happen to me, if I'm not careful up here.

Without vitamin D, I'd get eaten up by some kind of cancer.

Too much of that D, though, and my skin'll bubble up with cancer all the same.

The world's not a perfect place.

Ask Kid Hoodie, right?

Not because I want to but because it's time—he's past stiff, is just a bag of soup now—I put my big apron on and peel him up from the table, sling him across my shoulder. Sticky sweet air trickles from him at both ends, and a long string of wet from his mouth catches on the back of my calf.

I hitch him forward, push his chair back in, and carry him down the hall.

Not to my bedroom, but to the other room.

Back when, this room was supposed to be where all the action went down. I mean, I soundproofed it, made all the walls too thick to kick through, even beefed the floor and the ceiling up and fitted a drain and exhaust fan and fixed guards over all the outlets and drilled five spy holes.

All the things you pray for when you're young, they don't turn out to be exactly what you really wanted after all.

What I'm trying to say is that the only real way to get anybody back there, without them clawing at the walls and screaming the whole way, it's to dope them, or sap them in the back of the head, or at the very least bind and gag them. And that just takes all the fun out of it.

Want to play a board game, bub? Maybe talk?

Never mind the chainsaw on the wall. And no, that's not old blood on that drain grate. The door? Oh, it's only locked so nobody disturbs us. It's not to keep you in, not at all. These teeth? No, no, they're not to eat you, dear . . .

Yeah.

So what's happened over the past two years is that the whole apartment's what that one room used to be. It's the only way.

There's still the chainsaw, though, don't get me wrong.

I close the door before pulling the ripcord, then hit the vent hood first thing. Passing out from carbon monoxide while holding onto a live chainsaw's no joke.

No goggles, though, no beekeeper hat, no heavy duty gloves, and never any liquor. Not even a drop.

The first cut into Kid Hoodie is along the meaty outside of the thigh, the football filet I call it. Both sides, almost down to the bone. Then turn him over for his ass, just one straight angle down through the jello to the hamstrings, then the calves all the way down to the Achilles, which makes his toes rattle when I ride it wrong.

"Sorry," I tell him.

He just stares at the floor.

Soon enough he weighs half as much as he did, and that wasn't much in the first place, really.

I killswitch the chainsaw, flick the vent hood off, wipe the splatter from my face.

"Well," I tell him, studying all the parts of him on the floor now, or hanging off the edge of the rusted table, or collecting in a slurry for the drain.

My fingernails, again, are going to be crusted with leftovers.

I wheel the wet-dry vac over, suck up what I can and have to tell myself not to grit my teeth.

I can't help it, though.

It's because of this one dream I had early on, that involved the wet-dry vac. In the dream, I'd just walked into the living room, had this minty shaving cream still on my face, and in my mouth somehow, or maybe it was toothpaste, but anyway, the reason I'd stepped out of the bathroom was that there was a knock on the door. More forceful than usual, like whoever was out there in the hall knew that this was where they meant to be. Maybe even knew I was in here. Not that that makes any difference. I've had guys straight from lockup, and I've had guys with nightsticks. So, wrapped in my towel, just a safety razor in my hand I was maybe going to improvise with, I shimmied between the table and couch, was almost to the door when I noticed something wrong behind me.

It was the wet-dry vac. Just parked there by the television.

We stared at each other for a bit, me trying hard to remember if I'd had it out here for a mess, it just thinking whatever wet-dry vacs think, I guess, which probably has a lot to do with wishing they'd been better in their last life, and then I turned to the door again, for Mr. No Nonsense, Mr. I-Don't-Have-Time-For-This, Mr. Answer-the-Door-Already, but stopped, my hand to the chain.

A wheel creaking? A *caster*? Does plastic even creak?

I turned, just my head, some of my body I guess, and that's when I saw it: the wet-dry vac, it had *two* hoses now, like arms. And was definitely watching me.

And then the knocking insisted its way in, had been real, not some stupid dream. It didn't go well for the guy.

But then, yeah.

Does it ever?

Anyway, now the wet-dry vac's power cord, it's fixed to the wall with three clusters of five insulated staples. To anybody looking at it, they'd think I maybe just got tired of it coming unplugged all the time—some sockets are like that, end up with you pinching the metal ends so they'll grip enough—but the fact is, that power cord's only long enough for the wet-dry vac's accordion hose to reach all around this room.

No more dreams, either.

Mostly because I'm living the dream, I mean.

Ha.

After the wet-dry vac's over in its corner again, its belly heavy, I get the cat bar, pry all Kid Hoodie's joints apart. If you do it right, you don't even need a knife, really. It's like they're made to come apart. All you need's a little pressure between, then some twists for the cartilage and ligaments, and you're done.

Except for the teeth.

They come out one-by-one at first, with water pump pliers, but when I can't reach the ones in back, even after flaying the cheek and wrenching the jaw down, a hammer and chisel takes care of the rest. I pinch them up from the throat, have to cut a couple from the neck, and rattle them in my hand, want to throw them like dice.

I could probably sneak one into the Trouble bubble, I suppose. Make the game really matter.

But I've made promises to myself.

Each tooth, I hold it on a tailing of a railroad track that's an anvil for me, and I smash it with one of my dad's old spring-handled slag hammers. The thick molar from way in back has a bad cavity going on, too. Looks like I was doing Kid Hoodie a favor, maybe. Saving him some trouble.

I wash the fragments down the drain in the floor, the water from the hose lapping at my boots but they're oiled. My feet stay dry, always. That's a rule.

As for the bones, I braze them with the torch until the marrow bubbles up and out the little nail holes I tapped, then I turn the vent hood on again and light them with kerosene. While they burn, get brittle enough to grind down to powder like the teeth, I lug the wet-dry vac's tank to the kitchen, leaving wet tracks all down the hall. If I had a wife, she'd be yelling at me right about now: *You messing up my hall again, Billy? You think you're the only one has to use that damn carpet? You didn't get the cheap orange juice again, did you? Tell me you didn't, William C. Hughes.*

For obvious reasons, I live alone.

In the kitchen is the three-basin sink I had to special order, then install twice to keep it from leaking.

In the bottom of each basin is a garbage disposal. The first is the heavy-duty one, with the big industrial teeth. It shits what it eats straight down into the black pail with the good handle.

I feed Kid Hoodie to it then collect the pail, pour it slowly into the ammonia the second basin's already lapping with. There's just enough room.

After soaking for two hours, long enough for me to remember the kerosene, and to check the plug on the wet-dry vac, and to strip the skull—I'm weak, find myself looking over my shoulder, studying the mouth of the hall, for these two grey accordion arms to throw themselves forward, catch on each side of the wall, pull the red plastic body up with them—I flip the disposal under the second basin on, let it whir dry for a few seconds before pulling the drain, letting it all slop down to the smaller teeth, so dry, so ready.

They chew Kid Hoodie smaller and smaller, spit him down into their blue pail, and I pour it right back in without even setting the drain, only remember to kick the first basin's black pail over at the last possible instant.

Close call.

The last basin's already sloshing with bleach. I pour the frothy meatshake of Kid Hoodie in, and should let it soak but it's almost four so I reach under, unplug the second disposal—only two can plug in at once, with these breakers I've inherited—and jam the third one in its place.

I stand back while this disposal's fine little teeth finish the job.

Not because bleach might splash in my eye, burn me—I guess it could, though—but because the bleach and ammonia are poison together. People don't realize the dangers built into all this.

I turn the vent over the range on now, bury my mouth in the crook of my arm, and squint until Kid Hoodie's all the way through the P-trap, surging down some mainline in the wall for the bowels of the city, which'll shit him out into the river, I'd guess, which, for him, has a ferry up there in the filmy sunlight, about to tip over, break some mother's heart.

When I turn all at once to the hall, too, there's nothing there.

I knew there wouldn't be.

For the third time now, Kid Hoodie's cell rings.

There's a thousand funny things I could say into it, I know.

Instead I just watch it, wait for the call to shunt over to his voice mail, that I don't have the password for.

On-screen, it's just a name, *Mary*, and, as a joke maybe, the picture Kid Hoodie's made hers, it's this little mass-produced

Virgin, a halo wired up over her head, her base round and plastic and probably adhesive.

I'm holding the phone up, studying it, when there's a knock on the door.

I pull my lips away from my teeth.

I haven't seen my face in a few hours, but the same stuff lining my fingernails, it's dried at the corners of my lips, I know.

And the apron, and the boots, and the carpet. The smell.

A second knock, and then a claw scratching once down the outside of the door.

Just what I need.

On the way over, without even breaking stride, I reach up to the dummy fan, for the dusty little .22 on top of the blade with the one black screw, and don't have to check if it's got one in the pipe or not, and don't have to thread the silencer on like they do in the movies.

What you can say while pulling the chain back is *Hold on,* if you want.

I don't want.

Instead, I slide the chain back then just rip the door towards me.

The first thing I shoot in the face is the pit bull, already lunging for me, inches ahead of its line of saliva.

The second is the man with the rolled-up newspaper under his arm.

Some days you just don't have the time.

As for how a thing like this starts: say you're like me, first of all.

It's not as far a leap as you might want.

Have you never thought about it, how easy it would be? That you could get away with it. Say one night you're working late and then coming home by some route you don't usually take, some sad and illogical route, a grief-spawned roundabout nobody'd ever suspect, and you see Cheryl, and she doesn't recognize you now that she's into her new job in that other town, is just here for some grand reunion tour, hitting all the bars she used to haunt, one last ride on the never-go-round, all that.

For just a second, do you not realize that nobody knows where she is right at that moment? And that they don't know where you are either? And that, if you're suddenly behind her, making up a reason for her to step behind this building with you, she's going to trust you, right? You're just you, from her old job. Totally crazy seeing you here, now. But sure, yeah, I've got a minute, ha ha, all right.

What she doesn't see is that, as you're ushering her into that alley, your index finger is dragging behind, touching five evenly spaced lines in the brick, and pushing a little too hard into the grit, so it hurts, so this can all be fair.

After that—after that what you have is the magic.

What they say on the science channels late at night is that each decision kind of kickstarts a new parallel world, like a burp into another dimension. That each life is a whole branch of lives, of what ifs, of other choices, other lucks.

But there are bottlenecks too.

There's me.

I'm the point where the branches, the options, the decisions and possibilities, where they all come back together, where they slam into each other like particles in a seventeen-mile supercollider and blossom into some perfect shape, just for a moment. Something never seen before.

For a while I was addicted, yeah.

Fucking science channel.

And I don't think there's been a Cheryl either, don't worry.

Not that I keep drivers licenses or carve names into some bathroom stall or any of that.

Like I've been trying to say, I'm in this for the long haul.

Sixteen years and counting, baby.

The first thirteen, though, yeah.

I was thirty-one when I got saved.

And it wasn't at church, believe me.

It started with this lady I got fixed on one day, a yoga instructor, her mat always hooked over her shoulder. No particular reason I got stuck on her either, I don't guess. Or, no. At the time, the reason she looked good was that there'd just been two blondes in a row. And they'd been about the same height, could have been sisters. So, what this one lady had in particular, it was this long black hair. Down-to-her-ass long, I mean, like she was filled with oil and it was spilling out the back of her head.

Ladies like that never see guys like me, either. Not in a thousand years. Not in ten thousand.

Until it's too late, anyway.

I didn't follow her back to her place like I kind of wanted to, so I could step out of the pantry behind her when she went for a wine glass, get that priceless little gasp from her, and that's the lucky part of all this, really. If I had followed her home, I'd have seen the gates and the house and all of it, and maybe just reached down for second gear, eased on by.

You don't want to go to their houses, though. Somebody always sees. *No, I don't think she was having any rugs taken away that afternoon, I thought it was her stepbrother Michael, he has a blue jacket like that,* and on and on, right down to the tire tracks you leave in that one part of dirt by the road: *APB, all cars, suspect's in a Chevy minivan, ninety-two to ninety-four model.* Just wanted for questioning, but shoot on sight if your badge ends in an even number, or if you know somebody whose badge does.

You can't think of everything, but you can try not to be too stupid, anyway.

Look at Bundy, say.

You can be as bloody and as sick as you want, just don't do it where anybody can see, and never stay in one place long enough to start making the news.

It's what kept me in the game those first thirteen years.

But then Belinda. That was her name, the lady with the black hair and the limber spine.

Just for the rush, I took her on the sidewalk, right in the middle of everybody. Just brushed my hand against her wrist then latched on, pinching through into the deadspace, so that her hand flopped up, those long red fingernails so light on my forearm.

The rest of her pretty much collapsed.

Not because of some trademark ninja move or anything. I'm mostly American here, if my dad's to be believed. The reason she fell into me like she did was just because she wasn't used to being hurt. As simple and as complicated as that. And that pain inside your wrist right there, especially if you haven't worked packing meat with a dull knife for ten years, gotten your arms all ropy, it can floor you.

After she gave me her weight, all I had to do was guide her up against the wall.

Because there were people walking all behind us, in their own little worlds but ready to look into mine if there was suddenly this screaming thrashing woman in it, I did what I had to: snaked my head forward, pressed my mouth over hers.

The first thing I did there was the last she probably expected. I could tell by her eyes, how they saucered out. I made a seal with my lips, sucked out all the air she'd been planning to scream.

Next, before she could breathe, I bit down. Hard.

She didn't pass out from that, but she did get knocked a bit silly from slamming her head back, into the brick wall.

They do it to themselves, right?

After that it was a simple act to maneuver her into my car, then get her yoga mat too, so there'd be no definite place to start the search, no epicenter for the grid, the canvas, whatever.

Just drive, Billy boy.

Not too fast, not too slow. Her shoulder belt on, the windows up, all the tail lights in perfect working order. A cap down low in case any traffic cameras are on, the license plate just a temporary thing, but off the same model car all the same.

Like that, Black Haired Belinda disappeared into the world.

Except that's the wrong name for her.

Halfway back to the storage unit I had planned, I had to kind of bonk her head into the side window, remind her what a good passenger she was.

Only, when I pulled my hand back, her hair came with.

A wig.

She was as blonde as the last two.

I closed my eyes against the city, the world, all of it, and wanted to take it out on her but slammed the heel of my hand into the dash over and over, until the lady at the light beside me had to pretend she wasn't watching. I waited until she couldn't pretend, then wrenched the radio knob from the crashed-in plastic, flicked it into the floorboard, Belinda pressing back into her seat, away from all this. The lady smiled with just her mouth, like she understood.

How could she, though?

If I wasn't careful here, the walnut hair dyes were going to start running low all over town, if you know what I mean.

And that's not the kind of attention that helps.

"You're screwing this all up," I told Belinda, taking a corner slow and gentle, half my mind on the rearview, like always. The lady going the other way.

"You don't—you don't—" Belinda tried, but was snorting and crying and couldn't finish.

Bitch.

I decided then and there to keep her alive for at least forty-eight hours. Maybe a shock collar or two, for if she tried to make some noise. Or maybe just the tongue pulled out at the root, the blood collecting in her throat like she's drowning, so I could tell her to breathe, to control her fucking breathing, that's the secret to all of this, right?

I still remember all of it, yeah.

Everybody says it's the first one you never quite shake (Mark Dashiel-something, from the carwash), but for me it's Belinda, the last one. The last one from my other life. From before I died and went to heaven. Apartment 439, Chessire Arms.

You don't get to a place like this without dying a little bit first, though.

So it was with me.

Right when I was most alive, too.

I was squatted down over what was left of my yoga instructor. It had been two days. Her lips were in a jar, her tongue was in a twice-used rubber, and in her belly where I'd just put it was the little toy of a dog I'd found yapping in one of her bags. We were going to stage a birth was the thing. Then the door of the storage unit rolled up all at once.

I looked back to the line of suits at the door like they were what they were: an annoyance; an interruption. The guy at the back of the theater leaving the door wide open until his eyes can adjust, never mind the rest of us normals.

I squinted from the sudden light, jerked my hand up for a visor, and the little dog barked once.

Like that, a row of pistols settled on me.

Behind them, this long black eel of a car.

And, in the middle of it all, this one silver-haired man, shaking his head at me. No gun, but just because all the guns were his.

As apology, I held the dog up.

The man stepped forward, took it, stroked his hand down over its head once then held its head like you do a chicken, when you're about to pop it around. But then he didn't.

It told me he had some idea, how a body can fall apart in your hands. But that he also knew how to keep it together.

"I'm guessing you've got a knife in there somewhere," he said, nodding down to the floor.

I held one up and all the guns stepped in, right against my forehead, so that I almost wanted it, to see what it would feel like.

"Now now . . ." the man said.

His skin was perfect, his breath a dream, his eyes delicately lined black, like a stage actor.

I flipped the knife around, handle-first.

What the man carved from the back leg of that yelping little dog was some bullshit computer chip thing. A tracking device for if it ever ran away, for if anybody ever decided to take it hostage, or if Belinda, *his* yoga instructor, ever left it in her Porsche then forgot where she'd parked.

He dropped the chip, crunched it with his heel.

"Mr. . . ?" he led off.

I stood, looked him almost right in the eye—I'm five-eight, barefoot like I was—and lied.

He knew it but smiled anyway.

"Her name was Belinda," he said then.

"She didn't breathe right," I cut back, using my fingertips to show where the breath was supposed to come from in a yoga instructor: deep.

He stopped smiling, handed the yapping dog off.

"Now I've got to deal with her father, did you think of that?"

"You really loved her, you mean?" I said.

Two loyal hammers clicked back.

"She was a rare find in this city."

"So what are we waiting for here then?"

He nodded, looked down along his line of muscle, their sunglasses all the same exact black, their hair perfect.

"I was thinking we could just close this door again," he said, shrugging, stepping closer to me, so that he was on some of what Belinda had been leaking. It made her groan a bit. Some of it must have still been connected. "Close this door and do as the good book says. In recompense, of course. Justice. Because of course vengeance, it's not mine."

He shrugged. I didn't flinch.

"Do you think *you* could last two days?" he asked then, his face right up to mine, his right hand snapping back for a gun, Belinda's hand pawing at his shin.

With the boning knife straight up under my chin, our eyes locked, he shot down at Belinda four times until he found her head.

It popped like the watermelon it was.

What got to me worse than that was that he was doing this without shutting the door. Doing it out in the daylight. I guess because he knew if any cruisers responded to a shots fired call, he could do the same to them. To however many came. And still walk the fuck away.

As I'd been to Belinda, he was to me.

But still.

"I've had a good run," I hissed right against his lips. "Do your worst, bub. Here, let me—" What I did was take my index finger, already bloody, and trace a dotted incision along my side. "If you cut here, and angle it over the first time you touch bone, you miss everything vital. I can still live for three days like that. You can watch the maggots boil out if you want. Take some fucking pictures to jack off to later, and use the maggots as lubrication. It's an experience I wouldn't want to deny you."

He considered this, considered me, then rubbed his nose all at once, handed the gun back to a waiting hand, for delivery to some river or acid bath or property clerk.

"I think," he smiled, then nodded. "I think the punishment should fit the crime, as it were."

"So you did love her."

"I don't give you the satisfaction," he said back, and came forward with the knife, drove it right into the line I'd traced. "Like that?" he said.

I tried to smile, couldn't quite.

32

"A small price to pay?" he read off my face, then laughed, turned around, taking the storage unit in. "How about this. In two days I come back to this charnel house. We'll be locking it from the outside, of course, and renting all the adjacent units, and having a discussion with the manager. So you won't be disturbed. But, when I come back in forty-eight hours, I want this evidence, Belinda. I want Belinda gone, Mr. Williams."

"Billy," I corrected, letting the fake name go like a balloon.

"Billy," he repeated, his voice just as flat. "That was smart, using a form of your real name for the other one. Easier to remember, right?"

"There's no drain in here," I told him, about disposing of Belinda. "And I didn't bring my—"

He shook his head no then, and two of his Armani goons stepped forward, lifted me by arms to slam me up against the cinderblock wall.

"Actually, you did bring your—" he said, clacking his jaws—"your implements."

Like the gentlemen he was, then, Mr. Singer—in two days I'd know his name—pinched his slacks up and knelt down to Belinda, stroking the side of her face with the cup of his hand. Then he reached down to one of the hesitant, embarrassing cuts I'd made around her breasts, and he pushed his fingers through the slight heal, came up with some slimy meat that looked like a bladder but was probably the milk sac she'd been saving for someday.

When I wouldn't open my mouth, his goons did it for me, with a pry bar I had on the floor.

It cost me two teeth, and filled my throat with blood.

It helped that first mouthful of Belinda go down.

I'm a vegetarian now, yeah. Fucking strict, serious as a heart attack.

You would be too, if that's what you had to do in the dark for forty-eight hours straight.

When Mr. Singer came back, he let me in on what this was all about: one of his many properties had a vacancy. And, due to circumstances beyond his control, one of his most dependable men wasn't going to be with him anymore, it didn't look like. Alas alas, his arm over my shoulder now, his hand massaging the back of my neck.

"And?" I said, a flicker of hope in my eyes I couldn't help.

I was naked too of course, because I'd had two days to hide blades all over my body.

"Have you ever heard of the sand lion?" Singer said to me.

I narrowed my eyes. Between my cheek and gums on the right side was a razor blade. And in the thick callous of my heel. Crusted with some hard-earned semen into my pubic hair. Hidden in the wig in the corner, in case I got slung over there.

"What it does," Singer went on, "what it does is beautiful, really. It burrows back into the sand and makes this funnel right above itself, and then just sits there waiting, so that whatever walks by, an ant, a caterpillar, a grasshopper, it slips in. Lunch."

He stopped, came around to face me, so we could be sure here.

"I can be your funnel, Billy," he said then, for all the world like a preacher trying to steer me on the right path here. "I can have them knocking on your door, man."

"Them," I said.

He nodded, didn't need to say it, and instead of pay, what I got was an all-bills-paid, one flat forever, so long as I took care of business, no questions asked.

Like I said: heaven.

Like the milkman in a movie, I whistle to pass the time, dolly Kid Hoodie's thirty gallon drum through the cutaway door in the back of the closet, deposit it in the apartment just left of mine.

Same as always, it's the only one there.

What I picture is some wooden warehouse out by a swamp, the drums stacked two deep along the side wall already, just waiting for that next flood to come along, pull the whole place down, leave the entire burial ground bobbing in the water, finally gurgling under like the toxic waste it is.

In the drum is a cocktail of lye and acid and camphor and ammonia and baking soda and straight feces—mine.

Each disposal runs Singer about four hundred dollars, I figure, not counting my room or board and whatever transport cover he has rigged up for the drums. Plus the two grand or so he could be pulling by the month from the flats to either side of me, and the one directly above, and the three I asked for below as well.

What it does is put me at the heart of a five-story cross, one buried right in the center of the Chessire Arms.

I've never slept so well.

On the dry erase board beside the drum, I write down a list of the vegetables and supplies I'm going to be needing this week, then add a couple of blue movies to it too, just to keep up appearances. Real hardcore, underground stuff.

Like clockwork, I know they'll be on the counter in the empty kitchen tomorrow morning.

Some guys are just born lucky, I guess.

It takes two more trips to get Mr. I-Don't-Have-Time-For-This and the pit bull through the closet, the dog microwaved to kill any tracking chips. And yeah, it gets its own damn drum, just so Singer can get the report: *Three?* But, but.

He'll never call, never come by.

We talked exactly two times, and both of those were in the storage unit. The only thing connecting us anymore are the missing. And they're not saying anything.

Instead of bringing a dry drum back to my apartment with me, I kneel in the living room, cut up a square of carpet to replace what Kid Hoodie messed up. Usually I'll just put it on the list if there's none leaning against the wall, CARPET, even add an extra T on the end—it's comfortable for them if they can spell better, if they can explain me away by a bad education—but this'll match my place more. It's not an unlimited supply or anything, but it'll look good for a few days. Be a nice change.

If I want, too, I can put a G up in the corner of the board.

This is a request for a girl.

Not in the lefthand apartment like supplies, though she is, but knocking on the door like the rest.

Come in, come in.

If it's somebody Singer was getting fed up with for one reason or another, all the better, I suppose. Though I'm finding, now that I'm almost thirty-five, that it's the ones who aren't quite twenty yet that do it for me the way it needs to be done. When you're twenty, just out of high school pretty much, all I am's just one more trick to fake your way through before you can go back to being who you really are, another number to erase from the debt you've already stacked up. One more ride to forget.

You've got a lot to learn, I mean. And I'm nothing if not thorough in my teaching.

Maybe there has been a Cheryl, I don't know.

One of them around Christmas that first year, a gift I'm pretty sure, she was even the spitting image of Belinda, yoga mat and all, nevermind that Singer had already sent Belinda's dad knocking early on that first month. From what he said, I was supposed to be the guy who had some idea where his daughter might be. His last ditch longshot maybe-baby pie-in-the-sky wish upon a star.

The story I told him was that me and Belle—that's what Belinda was to me, for him—had been kind of an item for a while, back around last November. That, and this was just to rub it in, she'd even gotten pregnant on accident around then, but then cried and cried because it would disappoint dear old Dad. So we did the perp walk down to the clinic, on the condition that we'd have one the right way when the time was right. After she'd introduced me all around, and we'd got established on our own, all that.

What the dad did was sit there and cry into his hands.

I choked him with his own tie.

Don't let anybody ever tell you life's fair.

Not as long as I'm in it.

Six days later, shaky, so alone, nobody at my door, I'm crouching in the lefthand apartment at dawn.

This is when the ghost comes, with vegetables.

I've seen him once before, but that was from a hole I'd fingered in the wall behind my headboard. He never knew, and I plugged it back up, made promises to myself. If you're not supposed to bite the hand, then it's definitely bad news to force it down into the disposal, right?

But it's been nearly a week.

Yesterday I fell asleep in the sun chair and when I woke the index finger on my right hand was trembling, like it had been doing something especially secret. There wasn't anything crusted in it though, and it smelled the same, didn't taste any different. Unless my mouth had been in on it too.

After that, I was up all night.

I finally even got desperate enough to go to the other apartment, pet Riley in the dark. Then, as apology, I took a wire brush to the back room, and scoured all three sinks in the kitchen, and adjusted the toilet until the tank was holding the absolute maximum amount of water possible, so that the first time the flange lets those long brass bolts shift in its rusted hold even a hair, half a hair, there's going to be a leak.

Now I need to see somebody, though. Talk to them.

Otherwise I might fade into the wallpaper.

If it's been like this before, then I don't know about it. I mean, okay, if it's ever been like this since I moved into the Chessire Arms, got locked up here, starting punching numbers for Singer.

Before that, sure, weeks like these, they were the only way I knew weeks could be, really. What made it worse was that I had to pretend that nothing was ever wrong. I remember I had a circuit back then, though, of people I'd talk to, people I needed: Don at the tire place, Laney, two doors down with the dry cleaner, and all the way up the block, people who would pass the time of day when I needed them to. Let me know in their indirect ways that I was still here, that things were cool, level, hunky-dorey.

Carwash Mark, he was the anchor for a while, even, until he jacked his hand up in the works, got on workman's comp.

Finally I had to just go see him.

I didn't really know what I was doing then, but things worked out in the end. So long as nobody ever looks in that plastic cocoon behind the insulation in the attic.

Maybe I'll tell the Vegetable Ghost about it, confess about Carwash Mark, just lay it all out there, wait for a shrug, telling me one guy at a carwash couldn't have mattered. Or, not a shrug, but a nod, like that's what the Vegetable Ghost would have done himself. That he appreciates me, admires what I'm capable of.

In a frantic, neat line at the top of the whiteboard, above all the exotic dummy vegetables I know I'm just going to harvest seeds from, not even eat, is a line of G's. Fifteen of them, five threes, not something I'd waste if I wasn't serious.

And *broccoli* is spelled right, and *artichoke*, and I even wrote a persimmon on there, though I can't really think what one might look like, or if they're in season.

For me, as far as Singer's concerned, they will be.

Like I'd know the difference between that and a mango that wasn't ripe, yeah.

Fucking island fruit. It would just make me feel more marooned.

At ten past seven, the door of the lefthand apartment finally creaks the littlest bit.

No knock, no bell, no *Is anybody home?*

This should be nightmare fuel for me, yeah, a door opening with no advance warning. But I've got other fish to fry. They're gasping in my head right now. If I were a junky, I'd check into some methadone clinic. Except they don't have wards for what I need.

Or, they do, but I'd have to sneak into one afterhours, hide a nurse or three down some laundry chute, then walk down the hall, dragging a scalpel on the thick-painted handrail, so that those little curls of enamel paint crashing into the sterile tile would be the first sign that I was on the floor, that the night was about to begin, ladies and gentlemen.

You don't walk away from that kind of fun, though.

All you get to do then is break into a cabinet, shoot up one of everything there, then walk out the front doors, see if you're bulletproof now or not.

It's stupid, I mean.

Better this way.

Crouching in the space where the dishwasher used to be, watching the door open faster now, your heart stopping all at once when, instead of a loafer, a shin in pleated slacks, what you see is the dull foot of some great machine, come special for you.

Heart, beat.

Breathe. Let it all wash out.

An instant later the rest of that machine: one wheel, ten

inches high, solid rubber. Aluminum frame, canted back thirty-two proper degrees.

Not a machine, a dolly, a handtruck, a dull silver keg.

Behind it, a guy in a uniform shirt that matches the label on the keg.

This is Singer's cover.

The label on the keg is Something-Something & Sons Grease Solutions. Restaurant lard, used, to-be-reclaimed.

Except that keg, when he tilts it forward I can see it's more of a coozie, like an insulator for a beer.

The thirty-gallon drums slide right in. I can tell because the lip of one (they're always stay-away green) is peeking out right now.

For a few moments then it's completely silent. I can tell that every bit of the Vegetable Ghost's attention is focused next door, on my place. And then he breathes out through his teeth. This must happen every morning. I almost smile, but he's wound up enough he might hear my cheek muscles creak.

And then he sees the fifteen G's on the whiteboard.

Do they mean anything to him? Does he understand that it means one girl, now, fast, and not fifteen?

As for the rest of the list, instead of writing it down he pops the top off the drum on his dolly.

It's a produce market in there.

All the normal stuff I usually list, he sets it in the refrigerator, in the proper places. The persimmon he has to call about, though. When the digits on his cell beep, he studies my place again, waiting for me to hear.

My index fingers taps once on the floor, on its own, calling out to him, telling him to run maybe. The sound dies before it makes it to him.

"Persimmon?" he whispers into the phone, then that he's already ten minutes behind. That he's got to—

I reach around, thumb his phone off for him.

This is the moment he's been waiting for for three years.

For maybe twenty seconds I just stand there, my chest almost to his back, my breath on his shoulder.

The reason he's not turning around is that I'm the boogey man. As long as he doesn't see me, I don't have to exist. Or, as long as I don't have a face, I don't have to erase it from his memory. Sponge it up off the floor.

"They're grown exclusively in the Canary Islands," I whisper right into his ear. "The persimmons."

He nods, believes this harder than he's ever believed anything.

"And they're not delivered in unhygienic containers," I add, telling the complete and inarguable truth now. "Are we clear on that?"

He nods a little mouse nod.

"And forget the girl," I tell him. "I'll trade you for her."

Now I'm the one who can hear everything: he's closing his eyes, tensing his neck, the muscles all along his spine contracting, in anticipation.

Six days. Nobody should have to go that long.

"Tell me your mother's maiden name," I hiss.

He makes a noise that's not a croak, not a whimper, but takes a bit from both.

I have to say it again, louder, before he can swallow his tears.

"T-T-Ta—" he starts, but I push him forward, into the wall, tell him to write it. First, middle, last.

When he's too wound up to risk erasing any of my letters, I hock a wad a spit onto the board, reach forward with the heel of my hand, swirl that weird non-ink all around.

"Now," I tell him.

Instead of using the marker, like he tries at first, he just writes the name with the pad of his traitorous index finger, because the white board's all black already.

TAWNY MAINE GRIMES.

I laugh through my nose, a real laugh. It even spills out my mouth some.

"Bull*shit*," I say, clapping him on the shoulder. It nearly kills him, I'm pretty sure. "That can't—" I go on. "I used to bang this one old . . . I never knew her middle name was Maines, though. That from your granddad's side?"

He nods, can't stop.

His mother. Like we're even from the same world.

I could have told him I was his accidental dad, even, and he would have been nodding, would have even written me twenty-two Father's Day cards right then and there, I know. Or however old he is.

Not was, yeah. Is.

I take one loud step back, and when he realizes what he's being given here, the son of Tawny Maine Grimes lowers his head, angles it the opposite way, and follows his dolly to the door.

"Not even going to check?" I call after him. It's not a question.

He stops, nods, then turns the long way around, knocks twice on the lid of the drum he'd already left six days ago. A hollow sound.

"Restaurant grease," I say to him then.

He says it into the emptiness of his chest: "I don't know anything, mister."

"I know you don't," I tell him, and then he's gone, off into the day.

My six—no: seventh.

I rest.

To keep myself from playing with the help anymore, I give myself a project.

First the Vegetable Ghost next door has to deliver some supplies, though. One of the items, Singer had to overnight from a medical catalogue.

I can tell from the sound, too, that that there's at least four shuffling feet now: two hands for the dolly, two extra eyes for me. Probably four or five guns between them, and a lot of nervous laughter down on the street, afterwards. A few cigarettes sucked down to nothing. A will they should have already written.

Lifestyles of the dumb and luckless, yeah.

That could never be me.

They don't have my kind of discipline. Could never sit in their kitchen the rest of the day with a human skull ('For Pedagogical Purposes Only') on the corner of the counter, and mold clay onto the cheeks, mound it onto the chin. Roll snakes thick in the middle and delicate at the ends, to fold into lips.

Doing this with a real leftover skull would be asking for it. *No, officer, I don't know where Kid—I mean Jason Pease—went.* I didn't even know that was his name. Last seen here? I don't know. I think he said he was going to Indonesia or somewhere. Jakarta, Madripool. Wanted to test out his new quicksand boots.

Hey too, any chance you could you help me with my disposal right quick, here? Something seems to be stuck in it.

No thanks. I'm no suicide.

I do wonder about my retirement, though. I mean, dry spells like this—nine days now—you start to wonder.

It's got to go down one of a few ways.

The most obvious, and poetic I guess, would be to move somebody else in. Just a clean transition. All it would require is somebody standing on the other side of the door, a new tooth-brush in his pocket, his shotgun already pumped, vest strapped tight. I'd be numero unamo for the replacement, job number one.

The second way, to have somebody sneak in while I was asleep, it would never work. First, I've jacked with all the locks, made them my own, and second, the two cutaway doors and the trapdoor down—I've never been up, even though it opens onto the roof, supposedly, a vacation I haven't taken yet—they're all rigged for noise. On top of all that, I don't keep regular hours, so could very well be awake at three in the morning, when the knob on my door starts to turn.

I don't know.

Singer could gas me out, or torch the place for insurance. Send some crew over to blitz the place, swiss cheese the walls while the mouse inside scurries around from corner to corner.

And that's the happy ending.

The sad ending, I don't even like to consider it. But it's what he's maybe already doing: putting me out to pasture. Directing all his traffic elsewhere, to some other Chessire Arms. My groceries will keep coming, but my sustenance will have dried the fuck right up, so that, after a while, I'll have no choice but to go back to the streets, live like an animal.

Again: no thanks.

Aside from all that, he could always just tip somebody off, get my place raided, have me paraded across the national news, my face in a six-pack with Dahmer and Lucas and Bundy and the rest of the clown brigade.

I'm not smiling for that camera, though.

If you've gone nationwide, then you should be ashamed.

To live on that screen is to die the moment the jackoff on the couch looks away.

To *really* live is to waver at the edge of an open-eyed dream, so that everybody's always jerking their head around, sure you're there.

And they're right.

But sometimes you just let them keep walking, too. Give them their sorry little lives. Like they deserve them, like they've earned them.

And sometimes you just reach into the belly of a dusty beast, plant their face against the table.

Kid Hoodie.

His cigarettes taste like campfire dirt.

I sit in the chair he bought it in. Trying to get in his head's the idea. I wake his nearly-dead phone up and scroll the numbers and names, put my crusty old sweat jacket on and shrug the hood up over my head, try to stretch my legs long and careless beside the table. I sanitize the ear buds five times then plug them into his cute little player, can't get his music to roll.

It does feel different, though, to have a hood on, have these wires trailing up to the sides of my head. Like life support. Like I'm somewhere else, even in a crowd. My own moving little room, one big window to watch from. And with the cigarettes, I don't even have to breathe anybody else's air.

All you'd need now would be a pair of black sunglasses and bam, every security guard in the bank's talking about you on their handheld, every cruiser on the street's radioing you in, moms with strollers are turning into stores they don't care about and counting to fifty with their eyes closed.

Dumb shit.

I pull the ear buds down onto my chest, peel the hood and sit back down on the stool, stare into the cave eyes of the skull I've molded a face onto.

A fucking kindergartner could do better.

The only thing even making him look even a little human is that the skull's anatomical.

But nothing's easy starting out.

Carwash Mark? I carried him all over three counties for two months, burying him, unburying him, wrapping him, washing him, cutting him up more. Sure that everybody knew what I was doing. That they could smell it on me, see it in the way I kept looking away. That there was some concerned citizen tabulating all my gas purchases, drawing lines on a map with them, and keeping track of what I bought, and what I bought more of, to try to throw him off.

Things improved, though.

After a while a calmness can kind of rise up over you like a cold fog. It hardens your skin, clears your eyes, steadies your hand.

But don't ever let yourself start thinking that you're above everybody on the street, either. That they're bugs, you're the big shoe walking wherever you want.

Some of those bugs'll have guns and badges, I mean.

Or worse: long black limos, and that same calm sureness you have. Times ten. And the muscle to back it up. To bury you, not in a hole, but a five-story building over in the dicey part of town.

Don't think like that, though.

You can't.

The door down at the street's broke, maybe. All these luckless-ass people bunched up there, waiting to come see me. Meet their unmaker.

There will be more. There has to. That's the deal.

I tap the edge of Kid Hoodie's phone on the table and say it each time it hits: they're coming, they're coming.

Maybe the big man's just on vacation, down in the Caymans or something.

It makes sense that he wouldn't let anybody else be passing this address out. That'd be like letting somebody else hold your main gun, then turning around to try to pick a penny up from the hardwood floor, right after you've been cutting your fingernails.

I laugh a little at myself. How stupid I've been. How spoiled.

Before all this, nine days was nothing, would just make the next sweeter, more perfect. Anything closer than about five or six weeks would be dumb anyway, unless I was in motion, a traveling man. Then all bets were off, everything was opportunity. Like when you're a kid at the circus: none of the rules of the real world apply. Eat all the candy you can, until it makes you sick. And then eat some more.

I cringe at some of the stuff I've done, yeah. Not the doing it, but the chances I was taking, right out there in the open.

That's what a bad enough habit'll do to you. Get you stupid, thinking so wrong you can't even tell until years later.

Then too, if I'd been thinking right, I never would have snatched my yoga instructor from the street that day. Never ended up here.

Things work out.

Like this. The obvious answer to why nobody's at my door for nearly two weeks, it's what I was saying: Singer split town for some rest and regeneration, or to avoid some heat coming down, or to have a sit-down with some potential business partners. And when he left, of course he's not going to have called me. No contact, right? Right. All he had to do was leave the support system in place so I wouldn't starve, and the disposal cover too, even though nobody's getting disposed of.

Things'll pick back up here directly.

Retirement, yeah.

Guys like me, they don't get retired, not so long as they're producing. *Re*ducing, really. If they do retire, ever, then it's just that they woke up one day the same way a butterfly must, with no clue it was ever a caterpillar. And they walk away into the crowd. Or, they find a Riley and *then* step into the crowd, holding her hand. Disappear, and never talk about it again.

That's a long way off for me, though.

Discipline, discipline.

To prove it, I make myself sit on the stool by the corner of the kitchen counter again. The skull, the clay.

Instead of trying to make my fingers take orders from my eyes anymore, I pull the hood down to my nose, study the floor, and let my fingers remember the soft spots in Kid Hoodie's face. That look his mom probably called sweet when he was a kid, and guilty as hell. The way he'd flare his eyes at somebody, just after they'd turned around on him. How he'd hold his lips in an exaggerated pucker that, to anybody who knew him, meant he wasn't stoned, he hadn't been smoking, no, don't they trust him? Ever heard of a thing called forgiveness?

Yeah. Let's see Henry Lee do this.

After a while, kneading the clay even warms it up, so that it feels right, like Kid Hoodie's bleeding again. Like I'm shaping real flesh here. Molding a real person. I half-expect him to whisper something to me. That he was asking for it, yeah. And that it's better this way, really. That I have no idea the shit he was having to deal with, before he walked down my hall, sat down at my table.

I want to adjust myself, but don't need the clay turning to grey dirt on the crotch of my pants over the course of the day.

Time for adjusting later.

Maybe I will put that G back on the list in the lefthand apartment. YG, even. A whole string of them, like scissor dolls, pinned to the wall.

And—yeah. Maybe I'll save some of the clay, get the girl to let me put it on her face. So that the whole time, I can reach out with the side of my finger, change her to somebody else like flicking a switch.

Shit yeah.

And then I open my eyes.

My fingers are deep in Kid Hoodie's face.

Except it's not him. And it's not anybody else either. It's not even what somebody looks like after two or three years in the ground.

It makes me breathe hard, have to control it.

Twenty seconds later I'm standing where the stool was, that dusty little hatchet in both hands.

The whole time since he sat down at my table, all the days between, they're blipped away, gone, erased. The oily tendrils are feeling up the inside of my neck, cradling my thoughts, blacking them out, singling them down to a single sneer, focused right in front of me.

"Couldn't just play along, could you?" I say down to Kid Hoodie.

He just stares out at me.

I turn him around so he's facing away, thinking his tough guy thoughts, what a hood he's going to be when he grows up, what a pushover this old shut-in is, just wanting to play some bullshit ancient board game, how he's never going to be like that, man. *Never.*

"Got that right," I tell him, lower than before, and wind the hatchet up, backhand style.

And then there's a knock at the door.

Because standing there with a hatchet, my hands slick grey, my breath too deep for anything honest, because that's no way to greet somebody—nevermind that lumpy old skull on the kitchen counter, just a little project I'm working on in my spare time—I just stand there coiled up. Waiting for the next knock.

It comes about twenty seconds later. Maybe twenty-five.

Sometimes this is what I do. If the follow-up knock's half a minute later, which is polite, then I make it quick, with piano wire or a hammer or thumbs deep through the eyes. Like mercy. Ten seconds, though, well. Then we're in for a day or two of fun times, I'd say. Bring out the toys, let's make some noise. And twenty, that's kind of a no man's land there. It's saying to me that they understand I may not have heard the first, but they don't have all day here either, okay? Depends on what mood I'm in, really. If I've had my sun yet or not.

And then there's always the possibility of just one knock, one shave and a haircut and then somebody out there shrugging, giving up, slogging all the way back down the stairs, trudging the five blocks back to their car before the meter waves its flag.

That's unlikely, though. Not because of anything complicated about human nature, but because they know that they have to see me, in order to do or get to whatever's next. Otherwise they wouldn't have been given this specific address.

And yeah, I've considered the possibility of that one-knocker being telepathic, maybe. Of, the moment their knuckles rap that last time, them remembering some dream they had four (five) nights ago, then stopping with their skin to the wood, staring into the grain of the door, and making the good decision for once. Walking away, into some other life.

So far that's only happened twice. In three years.

That's not bad numbers, not at all.

And hell, for all I know, they walked down, their hands in their pockets so they wouldn't be tempted to knock on any more doors, and, with their shoulders up by their face like that, ducked into the street, got mown down by a bus.

May as well have stayed and had some fun.

Could be I'd baked a cake, I mean.

Or something.

And then I'm not breathing so hard anymore. I uncoil the hatchet, let it just hang.

That last knock, maybe the first one too, here's how it went: knock, wait; knock, wait; knock, wait; knock, wait; knock, wait.

Five of them, perfectly spaced.

It dinged a delicate little bell in my head, left it trembling with anticipation.

What I wanted to do, what I had to stop myself from doing, really, was tapping the back of the little hatchet on the counter five times, to balance. Like I was this hopeful lonely rabbit, slapping my foot to the forest floor then listening with my whole body.

Instead, though it didn't really count, I clacked my hind teeth five times. It's cheating, because that's so close to my ear that it sounds louder than it is, gets me more credit. But if you don't at least try to balance things out, then who knows what can happen.

Right now, I mean, the person out there knocking so evenly, it could just be a standing blob of fleshy jello, the only thing hard about it at all the knuckled grip of bones it's knocking with.

What it's waiting for is to see if all those even fives are going to build up out there, wash down over it, melt it into a homicide detective, or into my father.

If I can balance it out, though, counteract it with perfect symmetry, then those fives'll wash down and it'll just be another refugee from the world, looking for that gate to Hell.

Right here, I'll say, and step aside, usher him in, my eyes flashing like pennies.

And I have no rules for a third series of knocks.

It's never happened.

Unable to let go of the hatchet, I pad across to the door, stand at it.

Somebody's breathing out there. Shuffling.

No turning back.

For knocking so perfectly, though, for making me flash on a giant metronome out there, the round fist of its brass-handed arm reaching out barely enough to tap into the wood of my door, I promise to make this quick: swing the door open with my left hand, which is backwards, but then what the door'll swing open on will be the little hatchet, its notch just made for the bridge of the human nose. Never mind who might be standing down the hall, their keys hovering near their own door, their key a lifetime away from the lock.

Scurry in, children. Daddy's working.

Except.

Right when the web of my left hand sparks into the brass knob, my feet braced to pull the door back all at once, there's a sound behind me.

On the table.

Kid Hoodie's phone.

And the ring tone, it's all different now. It makes me pull my lips away from my teeth, like an animal.

Instead of the digital chirping it's done those three times, this is something custom, something plundered right from my fifth grade afternoons, that I haven't heard for years and years, not even in my head.

A television song.

Come and knock on my door, we've been waiting for you.

I don't pull the knob, can't now. Can hardly stand, even. The cell signal's passing right through me, from the hall to the table, the sound going back along that same path, from the table to the hall.

It doesn't ring again. I don't know what I would have done.

After the footsteps out there are gone I edge to the window, part the curtains on the right side.

Crossing the street, pursing her phone without breaking stride, is a white-skinned woman with black flames of hair. Boots with clacky heels, tight jeans, ruffled collar on a wispy shirt. Looking both ways but there's nothing coming.

Dashboard Mary.

Hello.

I don't write anything on the list in the lefthand apartment.

Instead, I wait for the sun to come.

Maybe that's why I've been thinking wrong. Not enough Vitamin D.

It takes forever, though.

But patience. I know waiting.

To pass the day, I retreat to the game.

Not Trouble or Sorry or any of the others in the cabinet, that would just remind me there's nobody here, but the other one. The one where I'm the main player.

What it involves is nodding myself into the belief that I've been recruited by the television networks. Just one at first, but then they all want a piece, and are willing to pay. It's not about the money for me, though. All I need is one glass-walled apartment far under the streets, suspended in a giant and secret old Cold War bunker, with no lights anywhere, so that when I look out, through my walls, there's just a blackness. And I have no idea how deep it goes, how long the trash I dump out the door falls before hitting anything. What happens when I flush the toilet.

I'm alone. Except for the remote, and the television.

Per my contract, I can never watch any show to completion,

but have to digest fifteen minute increments, so as to give each network its shake. They're paying for all this, after all.

And here's how I got to where I am: on the third strike (that they knew about) of my aggravated pederasty career, when I was all ready to smile cheese for the booking camera, bend over into Population for a few decades, this lawyer stood up, intervened. Without ever talking directly to me, but so professional all the same, he bailed me out, got me a reprieve of some sort, a delay in the prosecution that's turned out to be pretty permanent. Or else the bail went forfeit, was really my price tag.

Waiting for my trial then, for what I thought was going to be my trial, he trundled in some lackey from the network. Somebody they could burn if they needed to. Somebody who hardly even existed, except for the offer he had for me.

Deal was, they needed somebody with my particular tastes, with a palate refined by years of concentration, and hands-on kind of experiments.

We both knew what he was talking about here.

I smiled, leaned back in my chair, did my eyebrows for him.

My hands, of course, were cuffed. Because I might, at any moment, think of some perfect little girl, start jacking off.

You can't stop a guy who's committed, though.

I was Houdini to their cuffs.

But the offer.

The flunky's eyes were dead as a snake's, just watching me. I wondered if he was maybe a robot, even. If a boardroom of network executives were actually here with me, behind those controls. But he didn't really have to be a robot for that to be the case, either.

I tried to look deeper and the flunky's mouth twitched into a cute little smile for an instant.

"Well?" he said.

My expensive lawyer—the flunky's really, I suppose—was pacing by the door. The less he heard, all that.

Like he wasn't getting paid too. I wasn't going to be the only one going to hell, I mean. Not by a long shot.

Before that, though, I still had some time to kill.

As it turned out, years and years and years.

The problem the network had been having, see, was FCC fines. Not for obscenity or vulgarity or even indecency, but for *suggestion*.

So, to get it straight from the start, it wasn't about them being upstanding citizens, it was about them saving their bottom line. Them covering their ass.

Spending a little on me to keep the rest from the FCC.

What had happened was that some task force or neighborhood watch group or some shit had done a study on the viewing habits of all the so-called pedophiles arrested over the last two years.

The results they got were well-publicized, enough to wake the lumbering fine machine of public decency, the Federal Communications Commission: a solid two-thirds of those misprosecuted gentleman, their show of choice had been this one with a ten-year-old girl in it (the actress was actually twelve, but fuck it, right?). In interviews, they'd huddle forward and whisper something about her hips, the way she moved when the camera was at about desk level, and she was kind of aware of being watched, but not really making that big a deal of it either. That killed them, went right to their grubby little souls, made them forget themselves, explode into nothing.

At least that's how the report phrased it.

However, the studies eventually done on that show, and the rest, could find no single thing to avoid next time, in whatever show got the greenlight.

Enter me, connoisseur of all things young.

All you needed, really, was the right kind of eyes. The right predilections, the right tastes, honed over a lifetime.

For my part, I just needed my suspended glass apartment, the bunker all around.

For their part, they needed a single, 'low-resolution' (but I know better) camera fixed on my television chair.

And my cable box, it only feeds me kiddie shows, fifteen minutes at a time. Or any shows with any kids in them at all.

On the table beside me, under the lamp, is a backup remote, some paper towels (I hate tissues; they break all apart afterwards), and the Corn Husker lotion I cut my teeth on. The grit in it is like . . . well. It's necessary. Big meaty platelets.

So, what the network—the net*works*, now—do is hire somebody, maybe that same original flunky, to watch the feed. To watch me.

Anytime I start to get too interested in the show on my box, he's to mark it in his logbook. If it's even a he up there, I mean. Most times, I want it to be bring-your-daughter-to-work day, and for the dad to be on a coffee break, the girl to have been about to change the channel, but—?

I can put on a *real* show, I mean.

And, they think they're in charge, the networks, that I'm in some glass prison down there, serving the safe sentence I would have been doing topside, but they don't know anything.

Half the time, the lotion and the box fan going at once, I'm not even focused on the screen, but have ramped through that living room the sitcom family uses, are back in their bedroom, so like other bedrooms I've been in.

It jacks their data, alters careers, makes them change their whole programming schedule.

I change it, I mean. And that changes everything, at every level of society. Just me at the center of it all, hunched over in my chair, squinting with concentration, reality creaking into place around me with each individual stroke.

And still, every day there's food, whatever I want, and I can monitor my bank account on the computer (and not only that—they say I need regular outlets for my irregular interests, and have dedicated a line, one they say can't be traced), and the only trade-off is that I have to sit here at least eight hours a day, glued to the set. Connected to it by these long white strings, anyway.

Ha.

The only thing that brings me out of this, my thumb frantic on the remote every fifteen minutes, is that the sun finally slants through the window of the Chessire Arms, warms my left shin.

I look away from the screen, from the comfort of the game. But I bring those same eyes over with me. That feeling.

I'm in control again.

For two hours I let the world warm me, infuse me, the chatter from the television dying away, the sound of Dashboard Mary's heels—that I couldn't even hear from up here, but were all the louder for it—dying away too.

When it's over I stand, wait for the walls around me to shimmer into place. They're not glass. But the show that's on now, it's one I would have wanted.

So there's that.

I smile, flick it off anyway. Can call it back when I want.

"So," I say to Dashboard Mary, wherever she is by now. "You're my age, I take it."

How else would she know *Three's Company*.

I nod to myself, slip next door to spoon Riley some soup, clean her table, and then am back to my front door.

Not allowing myself to pause, and just to prove to myself that I can, I swing it open, can see from overhead, like this is a blueprint, the tight little sweep the architect designed for it to follow.

Everything according to plan.

Except.

There on the carpet, where Dashboard Mary had to be standing, is a thick little oblong book of sorts.

I get a flashlight, train it on the thin white cover, my thoughts so unpolluted right now.

The user's manual for Kid Hoodie's cute little phone.

I look away, close the door and pace from room to room slapping the walls, thinking, then going back, slapping each slap four more times, so it's really two claps leaving one slap over, which you can only fix by making sure you've done even sets of half-claps, so they all add up right, no singles left hanging to cup your face later, before you even realize it's happening.

And then I do it.

With gloves and sunglasses and a hat, and hanging onto the sleeve of one jacket that's tied to another that's tied to another that's tied to a squat little leg of the couch, wedged against the counter now.

I lean out into the hall, nudge this gift with the leathery back of my index finger.

When it doesn't do anything, I collect it.

Locked in the decompression chamber of the wet-dry vac, the user's manual of course can't do anything to me.

That lasts about four hours.

By this time I've cut the body from my sweat jacket, nestled the hood and shoulder down over the educational skull and tacked the cape part down to the countertop, even run the ear buds up and clayed them in place.

I don't have to see the face anymore anyway.

But the ear buds, it's stupid: there's no music piping through them. If I'm beeping around on his phone, he's going to hear.

Going to know that I want to know something in there. And that's when the power can shift.

And, would she have even known that his phone was still here? Just to check—you can't be too careful—I've scoured every last inch of my apartment. Not in advance of some forensic team, but to see how she could have known that I couldn't work that phone. Cameras disguised as buttons, buttons as listening devices, little sponges soaking everything up, tied to a fishing line so she can pull it back whenever she wants. But there was nothing.

It had to be a guess.

Better than that, even, an accident. She could have been carrying the manual for him, for Kid Hoodie, then, digging for her own phone in her purse, dislodged it, and not heard it fall. Not stepped on it when she turned to leave, that third set of perfect fives still closed in her hand.

I try to think of other things, of a dog made of butterflies, of a band named Spore, of what magazines I should consider subscribing to but never will, of how LED displays work and whether there's some greater plan there to trap me counting lines, balancing them against other lines, waiting for a perfect symmetry of display and time before I can ever do anything, but soon enough I'm shoulder-deep in the wet-dry vac's belly, prizing up the manual.

I set it on an ancient place mat I've never used, walk around the table biting my thumbnail.

Kid Hoodie watches from his place on the counter but doesn't say anything.

I would pry the nails up from his neck straps and move him, throw him away even, use a whole barrel to get rid of him, but he watches the hall for me when I sleep now. We've made a deal of sorts about it: if I eat what kind of cereal he likes, with too much milk like his mom used to slop in, then he'll let me know if there's ever any wavy robot arms in the hall.

You do what you have to.

But the manual, the little phone's bible.

I lower the crossbar over the front door, drop the pin through just once and squat there in the corner, open the book. Only allow myself to breathe when my head starts to cave in a little.

Two hours later I'm still staring at it.

This is what discipline is: reading the instructions enough times that you can leave the phone itself up on the table. If you have to get it down to run through the controls, understand *that* way what the words are already telling you, then you've failed, you're losing.

If, however, you can just picture the phone in your head, and get properly intimate with it that way, then when you come to it, you're master already. It has no choice but to do exactly what you tell it.

When it's done, when I know how to work the phone in its entirety, when every nook and cranny of its functions have been laid bare for me, I nod a single thank you across town, to Dashboard Mary, then set the manual down against the baseboard, pat it into place, thanking it as well. Gratitude is such an essential part of living, I mean. I don't deserve any of this, I know. And, if I ever start thinking I do deserve it, that something I've done has earned me this station, then that'll be the day I lose it all. With nobody to blame but myself.

Calm again, not needing to tap anything on the way, I cross to the table, lift the phone like it's just another thing. Because it is.

"Your girlfriend," I explain to Kid Hoodie, the wires from the player still trailing into the blackness of his hood.

Kid Hoodie just stares, doesn't nod thanks.

I chuckle at how stupid he is, then, like I know to do now, hold the off-button down for a steady five-count, to either turn the thing off or wake it up.

On cue, like it has no choice but to do, the phone alerts me that it knows what I want, some bullshit animation doing its tired cycle across the screen, but then, just the juice necessary to be pushing that light around like that, it pulls the battery the rest of the way down, so that the phone makes a sound like it's digging for traction, straining forward, trying to be good.

Except then the little indicator light blinks out, comes back red.

On the display, already fizzling, the power meter alert I know from page xiv.4b of the English section.

"Recharge," I recite.

It's the first fix on each entry of the troubleshooting list.

Breathe in, hold, hold, relax.

I do, even manage a bit of a tolerant smile.

Now Kid Hoodie's the one chuckling, back there in his shadow.

"Fuck you," I tell him, but don't rip the ear buds out either.

Instead I try every power cord in the place, then finally accept what I'm going to have to do here: cut the cover off the manual, tape it to the list in the lefthand apartment, then write CHARGER under it.

So demeaning.

I'm already ducking back through to my closet when I remember, go back, add LOTION to the list. They know what kind.

What I get instead, the next afternoon, is a girl. A young one.

It's not the first time this has happened—a kid, a young girl even.

I think Singer was testing me with the other one, though.

Testing himself, maybe.

Here's how it went: I was two months in, still waiting for that crack of daylight when nobody was looking. And it wasn't that I wasn't happy, it was that this was too good, it had to be a set-up of some kind. I'd done permanent things to his Belinda, I mean. What I was expecting was that he was going to use me to dispose of a few undesirables, then arrange for *my* slow disposal. You shoot the housekeeper when the room's good and clean, after all. The front desk'll send another by soon enough.

So yeah, my bags, they were still packed. Except that I didn't have any bags. When I'd moved in, I'd been wrapped in a blanket that wasn't even mine, that somebody in the hall pinched onto when I stepped over the threshold, so that it stayed out there.

The plan initially was for me to use the halls to go to the lefthand apartment for supplies, the other apartment for whatever—"Think of it as your summer place," Singer said, his hand all fatherly on my shoulder—then use the special elevator key to get to the two below if I needed, and the one above.

I'm not stupid, though. Neither are prairie dogs or ground squirrels. They grow up with sharp eyes always watching for them too.

I burrowed into the apartments on either side, tunneled straight down to the other two but just walked around them once, blinking over and over again, like taking snapshots. But it felt wrong, like watered down versions of my apartment. Pale copies. If I stayed there too long, I'd go pale too. To prove it, I had the Vegetable Ghost leave me six boxes of mannequin kits. I carried them down through the trapdoor one limb at a time, and then assembled five in the bottom apartment, the base of the cross. The one I made a kid's looking out the window, always. I've seen a guy in the building across the street watching the kid. In the kitchen the kid's big sister is on her knees, has her head in the stove. The dad's hanging by his necktie in the front closet, like he's just another jacket somebody shrugged out of ten minutes ago. The other two are just sitting at the table, waiting to eat something.

They're the ones I think about the most.

I can't go check on them, though.

The sixth mannequin has the plastic soles of her feet glued to the underside of the trapdoor in my dining room. Hanging by kite string all over her body are bottles filled with marbles. Mom. She never closes her eyes, will tell me the instant anybody gets too close.

If I pull it open hard enough, though, she'll shatter at the ribs, and I'll slip down through the hole, monkey across the handles bolted into the ceiling, be halfway through the other trapdoor in the bedroom, the one with the rug nailed to it for cover.

Now you see me, now I'm gone.

The best plan's just to not ever need to run, sure.

But you don't want to get caught needing to run and not having a plan. And I've done it in my head a hundred times:

running through that bottom apartment, touching each of the five mannequins on the lips with my index and middle fingers, in farewell.

And the look on their faces after all these years, shit.

It almost makes me *want* to rabbit.

But that was the Egyptian me. The one in the old days, who built everything. The one who had no idea what the volume was going to be, what kind of traffic to expect, or hope for. There just wasn't enough to go on, then. I mean, aside from Belinda's dad that first month, there'd been exactly four others: a guy who obviously owed money, and tried to pay it to me (I let him); one of Singer's goons, who tried to convince me to call Singer to make sure this wasn't some accident (either way, right?); a girl who claimed to be pregnant, like that was supposed to keep me off her (she wasn't; we both saw); and a pizza delivery kid. And I'm not even sure if the pizza was from Singer or not. Wrong addresses happen, after all.

I didn't eat the pizza. It had sausage on it.

I put it in the barrel with the kid, tamped the lid down with the rubber mallet.

It was a living, I told myself. All I needed was a time card, really.

Until that first little girl.

Her knock was all wrong—uneven, already scared.

I opened the door, had the long barreled .22 in my back pocket the way I used to do it, to be sure nothing ever got out of hand.

She was just standing there.

Maybe twelve years old.

My stomach turned over a bit. Not because I'd never done a kid, but because, weighted down from her neck was a badge, a shield. It hit her at about the waistband of her jeans.

Special delivery.

The dad, I had to assume, was already history. Leave the dirty work to me.

"They said he was in here," she said, leaning over to try to look past me.

I reached back for the solidness of the .22, the assurance, and stepped aside. "Yeah, right in—"

It's best to not finish your sentences, sometimes. It leaves room for people to walk in, try to finish it themselves, by looking into the kitchen, down the hall, their eyes shaped like they're just about say something.

Behind her, I let the door swing shut.

She stopped when she heard it.

"Dad?" she said, into my apartment. Her voice just hung there, filling every empty space at once.

This is Riley.

What I've done for her is a kindness.

And the girl at my door now, a lot more Y than I mean when I put YG on the list—not that I'm complaining, mind you—she's the same all over again. Except for the outfit.

She's a Girl Scout, right down to the clipboard.

My mouth twitches into a smile. Wholly on accident, which is rare. You'd think I'd know better by now. I mean, the wolf, he didn't lay there in grandma's bed with saliva running down the base of his jaw, did he? Never let them see your hunger. They can use it.

"How'd you get in here?" I say down to her, my hand still to the door like I'm maybe going to close it here. Like I'm one of those people.

"I just—" she says, leaning back to point down the hall, and the way she leaves her sentence open at the end, *my* trick, I lean out, look down to the dull door of the elevator. Lean out far enough that anybody hiding to my left could have sapped me if he'd wanted. Scooped my brainpan clean, licked the backside of my brow ridge.

Stupid, stupid.

I grip the door harder, try to funnel all my mistakes into the muscles of my fingers, the clamp of my hand.

"I'm with Girl Scouts," the girl starts, reading from a laminated card in her mind, "and my troop—"

"How much?" I interrupt, playing for time.

Did she just catch a lucky door down at the street, start working the Chessire Arms from the ground floor up?

"For . . ." she leads off, parentheses around her eyes like a character in a cartoon panel.

"Three boxes, say."

She does the math, moving her mouth around the numbers, then comes back to me: "Twelve-seventy-five. No tax."

I nod like this is a cheap enough way to get her to leave, sure, then turn. But the door starts to swing shut between us.

"Hold this," I tell her. "It locks automatically."

Hesitantly—I'll give her that—she steps into the door's little arc, leans against it with her shoulder.

Oldest fucking trick in the book.

I go to the kitchen, touching three things on the way then the counter twice, and dig in the drawer, all the time humming a song to myself. Because I'm just this innocent, lonely guy. A little gruff around the edges, but probably diabetic too, unable to say no to thin mints.

I come back with the cigar box. Lots of people keep house money in something like that.

And I'm maybe wearing wire-rim sunglasses now too, and a black cap pulled way down.

Probably, yeah.

They were beside the box, from last time.

The Girl Scout's eyes widen in the most perfect way, and she forgets all about her lips, her sale.

In her head, I know, she's telling herself that she's in the hall, practically. That I'm old and she's young, so she's faster.

That she never should have come here.

She's right.

"Oh, this," I say at last, touching the brim of the cap. "The light—it's nothing. How much again?"

My fingers are in the cigar box now, our transaction almost over.

What the Girl Scout can't see is that what I've got in there's a hypodermic needle filled with drain cleaner, two broken pens and one functional one, a piano wire tied to two porcelain cabinet handles from the bathroom, and three of the big cat-eye marbles I used to covet as a kid. They can work as eyes, if you push them in but not too deep, and especially if there's a candle anywhere in the room.

All of which is to say that I'm not going to let her get to the table. It would be a betrayal. Riley would know, would hear it in the way I breathe. Or worse, hear the girl's voice through the wall. It's why I'm wearing the cap and the glasses, really. Because I have to think that Riley's somehow flopped over to the wall, is watching through an electric socket or something. Thinking she's not the only one anymore.

It hurts my soul to even allow that possibility.

I shake my head no, for Riley not to worry. That I'll make this fast.

Piano wire's what I'm thinking, what I'm already untangling, what the Girl Scout would *know* isn't money if she were more than ten years old and not about to sell *three* boxes, and I've just got it out enough to loop over her wrist if I'm fast enough, the one she's holding the clipboard with, when suddenly, and with no warning, she's not alone.

Behind her a shape, a woman, a voice. It shatters through my head. I don't look up, keep my head down like a servant. Just watching the Girl Scout. The woman suddenly and undeniably framing her.

"*There* you are," Dashboard Mary is saying from a hundred directions at once, her red-nailed fingers protective on the girl's shoulder, her voice half a scold. "But, what floor is this?"

The girl jerks her head up for my door number, caught.

"That's right," Dashboard Mary says—I can smell her, taste her on the air—"I'm sure I told you he lives on the *third* floor."

"But you, you said—" the girl starts, and Dashboard Mary reaches out with a porcelain hand, to guide my hand down. As if pushing money away, no, no. Like she doesn't even see the piano wire looped up past my fingers. Or maybe she thinks it's the wire you hang pictures and mirrors with. That this cigar box is my version of the junk drawer.

Or maybe she really and truly *doesn't* see it.

I don't know. She's still just a waist, a pair of legs. The same clacky boots.

"An honest mistake," she says to the top my cap, my eyes so wide behind the dark plastic lenses, like a rabbit's. "She's only supposed to go to people she knows . . ."

I nod with her, my head going even lower. "Safer that way," I intone.

"Can't be too careful," Dashboard Mary adds, opening the palm she has on the Girl Scout's shoulder in a way that means she's talking about all the slobbering freaks the city must hold in its thousands and thousands of rooms.

Not me, it means, standing there without a face.

Me she accepts.

I haven't breathed in a while now.

"Now, Megan, if you'll just," she says, turning the girl around, directing her back down the hall. "We're so sorry to have bothered you," she tells me as goodbye, hushing her voice down a notch or two, her steps small to match the girl's, and I know all at once that the whole time she was standing there she was trying to decide what I was staring at. I follow my own eyes down to what she must have seen, the ankle rig, and nod like I deserve this, yes. But it's our secret, me and her. She didn't say anything, at least.

Only when she's gone does the name stitched onto that Girl Scout uniform resolve some, like a Polaroid developing, coming into focus.

I can't get all the letters, but it started with an A, not an M. And when the Girl Scout looked at the numbers on my door, she looked at them with her eyebrows up, like they were the *right* numbers, right?

I don't know.

Once their footsteps are gone, I push the door shut, have no doubt that Singer bought ten boxes from that Girl Scout. Twenty maybe. Because he knows her dad, works with him, or against him. Or used to. Before he leaned down and whispered to her about this one guy who would probably buy all the rest of her cookies. This one guy over at . . . something 'Arms.' *Chessire*? Like the cat in the story, right?

I loop the piano wire around the index and middle fingers of my right hand, apply enough pressure for the nails to splotch purple, for the skin to split into a line of blood.

It's not enough.

The next morning when the flunkies dolly their precious barrel through the door of the lefthand apartment, I'm waiting for them. Have been all night.

I come down from the wooden pegs (used to be a closet rod) I've set deep in the wall and, before they even understand what's happening, I have the first one, the protection here, cheekdown against the floor, a ten-inch metal rod about an inch deep into his ear, the arch of my foot at the other end of it, no real weight on it. Yet.

He pees and the floor's not level here, so it streams across the linoleum, gets to the dimpled brass edge of the carpet.

The other guy, the one who inherited the Something-Something & Sons Grease Solutions uniform, he slowly tilts the dolly forward until the barrel's flat on the ground. Then, his hands laced behind his head, he lowers himself to his knees, places his forehead to the ground, maybe an inch from the pee. Because that's the very, very least of his worries.

"Is it in there?" I say to the guy under my heel, but he can't make words anymore, or maybe can't hear mine.

I look to the other one, the Vegetable Ghost.

"You."

He winces, peers up. Not quite at me, but at my knees anyway. Put those in a line-up, yeah.

I say again to him, kindergarten slow, "Is it in there?"

"W-What?" he manages. "The—the . . ."

"Show me," I cut in.

Moving with that same slowness that he thinks is going to save his life, he stands, his back never to me, and pries the lid off, starts to reach in.

"No," I tell him, and wave him over.

He's there in a shuffling instant.

Moving with a slowness he'll understand, I take my foot from the rod in his friend's ear, nod to it.

Instead of shaking his head no like I expect, he puts his foot up where mine was, like I'm showing him the first step of a stairway he's just going to have to trust me about here.

"You've got to give it a little pressure," I say, touching his knee with the back of my index finger, "just until you can feel—it's like stepping on a balloon, but you don't really want to pop it until the lady walks up the path and you can scare her right, see?"

He does, and steps down a little more, the guy down there squirming, his palms flatter than flat against the linoleum, his lips saying something. Nobody cares.

"Good," I say, "now don't—" but am already at the barrel, in it up to my shoulders.

There's the usual—vegetables, videos, baby food, the Sunday paper with all the date corners clipped off, put in a plastic baggie like puzzle pieces—and then, down at the bottom because it's heavier, a black bag from the electronics store.

Yes.

I dump it out on the counter.

The cover I tore off the manual is there, which means whoever went to the store took it with them. Good. But the charger, it's not the one specified for Kid Hoodie's model. I remember. Very specifically.

I slam my hand into the counter so that everything jumps. Especially the Vegetable Ghost.

It pushes the rod down deeper into his friend's ear canal, up against the sac around the brain, I'd guess. Just a touch, but when dealing with the human head, a touch can be a fucking mile.

"What's this?" I say, holding the charger up.

The Vegetable Ghost swallows, balances, tears running down his face now, and finally gets it out: "It has—it has adapters, the sales guy promised . . ."

He stops because I'm already studying this wrong charger.

In the hard plastic at the bottom are a cluster of alternate fittings. Adapters. It's a universal recharger.

I huff some disbelief out through my nose.

"What'll they think of next?" I say.

Now Vegetable Ghost shrugs, his eyes closed.

"So he promised it'd work, you say?"

He nods the truest nod of his life so far. Enough that I nod with him, even.

"May be," I finally say, weighing the charger in my hand then leaning over to him like we're best friends here, good enough buds that I can mostly whisper the next part: "Let's hope it does anyway, right?"

Instead of having him step down on the rod with all his weight like I'd had planned, I let him bundle his friend up, stuff him in the barrel, tamp the lid down. Then I take the rod, set it right at the lip, and tap it down once, hard, for an airhole. Maybe bloodhole too, if my aim's off. But that's all for later, and for them to deal with, not me. Right now I just nod to the door, that it's time to leave, then put all the vegetables in their proper places in the refrigerator, then study the charger some more.

May be, yeah.

Outside, in the hall, the sound of the dolly's wheels on the carpet are like thunder far away. Something building.

I count to five three times then duck back through my closet, lock the door behind me.

In the sunlight, my hands relaxed over the arms of my chair, I hold the little phone to the side of my head, listen to what Dashboard Mary's given me.

The manual says to let the unit charge to maximum capacity before operating it, to promote longer battery life. But the manual never allowed for me.

None of them do, really.

And it'll work if you just plug it into the wall. Even a kid would know that.

For the first ten minutes of sun, the wide dusty beam scanning up from my feet to my fingertips to my bare stomach to the thin skin stretched over my sternum, all I can access on the phone are Kid Hoodie's phone numbers. A trail leading all the way back to Singer, probably. Stupid fuck. But Dashboard Mary's in there as well. And the contact "911," which must have been their code or something. The ringtone associated with it's the Come-and-knock-on-my-door one.

I hiss, thumb past it.

There's a few songs too, what must be the soundtrack of Kid Hoodie's life, that he can thumb on each time he enters a room, so that it must feel like it's washing up behind him, like he's on some big screen, is doing something grand and noble and just a little bit dirty.

You tell yourself what you need to, I mean.

When you're as empty as him, at least.

And the music, it's about what I suspect. No melody, no heart, just a deep thumping in my head. A replacement for the heart he never really had.

Still, though I warn myself against it, I find my head bobbing with it a time or two, have to pinch my thigh hard to remind myself who I am.

The next time I forget, lose myself in it, I'm going to get the pliers.

This is what I threaten myself with. What I make myself stay awake with.

I haven't had to use tools on myself for years now.

But there was a time, yeah.

If I jam the dull jaws down into the flesh of my thigh now, where the hair's grown back over wispy and long, I know that what I'll be twisting will be hard little knots of scar tissue. From when that was the only way I had to get control again. When I knew I couldn't go down to the streets for another week or two, since the last puke had made the news.

And what you don't want to do if you can help it is ever get in a cycle like that. It doesn't end well. The only good ending to holing up like that, waiting things out, is that you live to do it all over again in some other town, some other state.

So I listen, and I don't nod, and I don't tap my index finger. And I remind myself the whole time that I'm not him, not Kid Hoodie, that listening to his stupid music doesn't make me him. That that's not what she's trying to do here, Dashboard Mary.

And then the phone serves up something new.

Not music, but a voice.

Mine.

You're him? I'm saying, two weeks ago.

I can feel my heart slamming in my chest.

I lean forward too fast, so that the wall goes splotchy—all the sun-warmed blood rushing up my neck, flooding behind my eyes—and thumb desperately for the menu behind this one.

I find it, open one of the arrows that branch off the current track, and there now, flickering from the effort of having to refresh—this is explained in the manual, is nothing to call customer service about—is a line stretching across the bottom of the small screen. A line with a stubby bar at each end, and with a right-pointing triangle way over to the left.

Because the green button's the control of about everything, I touch it lightly.

The triangle stands up into two pause lines.

I breathe out through my nose, close my eyes once, then open them back.

This is chapter 6, "Recording Voice Memos."

I angle the phone over. Right by the headphone jack is the little microphone grill, like a whirlpool sucking all my air down.

I push the stop button now and hold it like I mean it.

That prompts up a save option. I take it halfway, get dropped into all the voice memos. They're organized by date. A whole stack of them. Enough that they need a scrollbar, even.

The top one is the most recent.

I select it, look away.

To nearly two weeks ago.

You're him? I say again through the headphones, to Kid Hoodie.

Shuffle shuffle, look around.

This going to take long? he says back, his voice louder, closer to the microphone. Like he's meaning to talk into it.

I lean forward, look back to my counter.

Like I knew, Kid Hoodie's staring directly into me. Talking straight into my head.

Your ride? I say to him, back then.

Dashboard Mary, sitting down on the street, double-parked maybe, except that would draw too much attention. Circling, then. Over and over. Her phone open on the seat beside her. Her man upstairs, getting into Trouble. Upstairs on the fourth floor, number 39, like the strip of paper read.

Meaning she saw it, was his safety, Kid Hoodie's letter-to-be-mailed-in-case-anything-happens.

And the recording doesn't stop until the batteries wind down two days later. In voice-activation mode, that comes to about three hours of listening—each time I made a noise, the microphone opened up again, started sucking the sound in.

Mostly it's television, shows I recognize, and me asking Kid Hoodie about his cereal concerns. My voice is mumbly and slurred, hard to pick up. Like I've just thawed out of the iceberg, haven't had to talk to anybody for ten thousand years.

Behind all that, though, when I'm asleep either on the couch or in the bedroom, the recorder blips on for four seconds in the dark of the dining room.

It's just the lightest squeak, the slowest rolling.

Casters, I know.

The wet-dry vac has four of them.

"Shit," I whisper, and then erase it, then stare out my window long after the sun's been gone.

If I were some weak sister and going to stage a dream about Dashboard Mary, this is what I figure it'd be: her walking down my hall, up out of the darkness. Normal-length hall, normal no-lights kind of darkness, no invisible orchestra swelling up behind her. She'd just be looking straight ahead, her steps all even, no hesitation.

What she'd be wearing's her ruffle shirt, her tight pants, her clacky boots. Something cupped in the heel of her hand, but I wouldn't know what until later. That it's already there though would mean that I'm not one of those losers who make the dream up as they go, pulling in the car horns outside, the drippy ceiling, the smell in the air from the closet (decay), whatever they need to random things up. No, mine happen all at once, self-contained, complete, and then unfold as they go, with intention. Rooms exist before I walk into them, I'm saying. It's all waiting for me.

But one thing I do the same as everybody else, I suppose— maybe because I'm the one whose head this would be all happening in—is see her when I shouldn't be able to. In the hall, I mean. Not really through the walls, but clear as day just the same.

Each time her heel strikes the ground, the little green light on my ankle winks, so that it's like she's stomping the bulb out. No, blotting. Like she's stepping *between* it and me, even though

I can't get my pinky between the rig and the skin stretched over my ankle.

And then shuffle shuffle, skip a step, smear a nodded hello past, the way you acknowledge the plague when it comes knocking, and there we'd be in my apartment. No stupid pizza jokes, no fake flower deliveries, no Trouble. Just me trapped now in my chair, the sun so heavy on my skin. Her standing beside me, her left hand on my right shoulder like we're posing for a portrait, the painter in a window of the building across the street, so he has to study us with a scope on a tripod. Because we're contagious. But he can't look away, either.

Neither could I.

"Alison," she would say then, which would mean she was telling the truth now, calling Girl Scouts by their proper names, and I would swallow loud and then forget how to breathe for a moment, sure that I can hear her ruffled collar scrape as her head turns to the left, the kitchen, the counter, her boyfriend there from the neck up.

"An honest mistake," Mary would say then about having ever said Megan, gripping my shoulder for emphasis, the way people at church will squeeze your hand a bit harder at the *amen* part of the prayer. Like it needs that to stick. Like they really meant it, what the preacher just recited into his clip-on mike.

I wouldn't apologize to her, though, for Kid Hoodie. For her Jason Pease, her officially missing person. Her reason for being here.

Right?

Anyway, I *don't* apologize. That's another dead-end road there.

And that she'd cue into the way my hand on the arm of the couch would be balling into a fist would be a given here, I think. All her attention, I mean, it's on me.

"Can't be too careful," she'd say from above, her eyes unfocused too, to try to see farther through the window, through our sudden reflections—it's night for a few moments—and then reach down to cover my fist with the porcelain white of her hand, and pat it twice, like consolation. Like we agree on this, like we *have* agreed, like we've been agreeing, like it's settled now.

And it would work. It would flush straight through me, my pores opening to drink her touch and pull it into the branchwork of my blood vessels, my capillaries surging a thousand ways at once, deeper and deeper, until it's as if she's reached in, wrapped her fingers around the flare of my ulna.

At least until she lifts her hand.

That's when everything slams to a standstill.

If not for the sunlight, I never would've seen it.

But now I can't unsee it. Should have been seeing it the whole time. That way I might be prepared.

Glinting on her wrist, dangling on a bracelet, is what she was holding on her walk up the hall, what she's learned to keep quiet. It's the smallest little bottle. One of those little old prescription bottles like you find if you're running around the backwoods and stumble onto a fallen-down old house that everybody gave up on fifty years ago, that the great grandkids will never know to come look for, even.

About ten yards away from the back porch will be a mound of sorts. At first you'll think it's a cellar, that you shouldn't step there, but then it's the trash pile. Dig down far enough through the grass and wire and your fingers come up black from fires a century old.

In that black you can usually find the prescription bottles, the ones that were glass so didn't burn, and that didn't have big vulnerable sides to crack open every time the bucket or barrel was emptied.

It feels like stealing from the past, a little, can be beautiful, and that's why a woman would want to tie one around her wrist. Especially if the house had been her grandmother's.

The one on Dashboard Mary's wrist, though. The one she couldn't know to wear unless she'd seen the underside of my trapdoor, my mom upside down there, watching for me even when I sleep, because that's what moms do.

What I would do in response to it, to this chrome marble tinkling around in the bottom of the bottle like the most impossible pearl, would be to push myself as deep into the chair as I could, away from her touch, and then, when there's the smallest knock, from the cutaway in the pantry that leads to Riley's, I would wake gasping at the kitchen table, fall onto the floor and push myself with my heels into the corner by the front door, the new carpet coming with me, bunching up behind me, beside me, all around me.

If I was all weak sister like that, I mean.

If I gave in to that kind of shit.

I'd have been burned a long time ago, though, were that the case. Staked out on a stick and left for the birds.

What I do instead is just stand in the kitchen and stare into the stainless steel of the sink for a personal best, four hours. Then, to prove that the world's still on my side, I stuff my hand as deep as I can down into the middle disposal. All the way up to the forearm, baby.

You don't just hope the teacher's going to see it in your eyes, that you know that answer. You fucking stand up and scream it at her.

"Okay," I say, and lean over, flick the power switch.

The disposal under the third sink whirs on, grinds air.

"Exactly," I say to it, then push the couch up against the front door, go to sleep for real.

The next morning I hear the metal numbers on my door changing.

I have no idea where I live, nothing more specific than fourth floor, Chessire Arms. What some would call hell, I suppose.

Hey, I try.

But the Number Ghosts, they're not due for another week.

Does Singer think the Girl Scout's going to rat me out? Scurry back to her den mother with . . . what?

Like she was even a Girl Scout in the first place.

The more I think about it, the more I see Dashboard Mary down in the lobby, winding some fist-sized key into the back of this little toy she's made, so she can march her up to my floor, usher her down the hall.

Maybe it's what I get for not getting a little girl mannequin to go with the family downstairs. For putting the sister's head in the stove. Never mind that it was accurate.

But thinking like that takes me slapback to that dream that never happened, to Dashboard Mary running her fingers through the dust of the apartment below me.

She'll never know me. Not like that.

If the Number Ghosts aren't Girl Scout fallout, though, then that can only mean that they're early this month because of what Singer would probably call personnel problems. Somebody talking, that is. Making a face like they're going to talk, anyway. Probably one of the bar hounds who pass the slips of paper with my address on them, they got pinched, are sweating it out under some hot lights in a cinderblock room with one mirror.

Aside from Singer, I mean, those boarhounds, those girls with the unbreakable hearts, the grown-up boys still trying to live out the lives they planned when they were fifteen, they're the only ones liable to ever whisper Chessire Arms down at the station. The only other people who know that address, they don't have any teeth in their mouths. Or mouths, for that matter.

Maybe one of the boarhounds got religion. Maybe one of them finally figured out that giving somebody that piece of paper with my address on it's the same as pulling the handle on a guillotine (I'm the blade), the same as throwing a match on somebody soaked with gas (I'm the fire), the same as pinching some nursing home resident's oxygen line (I'm the one who gets to be with that senior citizen for an hour before anybody gets there).

But if some raid goes down, yeah, it'll be me on the news, I know. Not my support staff, not all the ghosts that keep me going.

Really, maybe the reason I'll even be on the news is because they found me with a scythe, standing in a pile of people who used to feed me, house me, lick my boots.

Or maybe it'll be Dashboard Mary who turns me in.

My chest goes cold again.

I smile the smile I try to always smile when I'm in the game, when I'm in the glass apartment and know there's a camera trained on my every move, and it's supposed to be fake, my smile, but this time it's faker than usual, fake enough that it wraps back around to the real.

This isn't a game.

I look down at the ankle rig blipping its lime green eye and know she's out there in the city right now, walking down some sidewalk, some mall, across some living room.

Finally I have to cut a square of electric tape, push it down over the light. Because I can't look away from it anymore. Because it's bleeding me right down into the machinery. Turning *me* into a ghost.

I could disable it if I wanted. I know that and Singer knows that. Most house-arrest flops—and this is the same model off those same police shelves—they try to pry into the works, or to soak it in enough carb-cleaner that it'll kind of just fade off the radar, but there's a reason their judge slammed that gavel down on them.

With me, it's different.

If I wanted it disabled, if I needed that light to get all weak and thready for forty-five minutes or so, I'd use magnets and speaker wire and a microwave, and if I wanted it off I'd starve myself down almost to dehydration then get the cooking oil, see what I could slither out of, what I could cut my way out of, what I could creak my way through.

If I wanted.

But I don't.

The real reason it's on is that Singer doesn't want me coming for him some fine day.

As for where I can go: all the way down to the elevator, and about halfway to the elevator on the floor below, and half that long on the next lower floor, with ten seconds of blinking yellow to give me time to come back to the menthol, baby, step into the green.

What this means is that I'm walking the inside of a globe. My world, yeah. My rules. And the core of it, that central antenna, it's most likely in one of the apartments across the hall that I've never been in. One of the apartments my cover people live in without knowing they're cover.

With all the metal holding the Chessire Arms up, I'd guess there's boosters too.

And—and somebody at Singer's palace or mansion or estate or penthouse or whatever he has. Just watching the blinking green cursor I am.

And you wonder why I play the game.

Sometimes the way I see it, through the eyes of whatever puke has to watch that radar screen, is that I'm the green cursor, and whoever's knocking is the red one. All I do, really, is smear the red one around some.

It makes me laugh.

I walk in perfect squares to the kitchen, skating my palm over Kid Hoodie's hood, and come back to the window with a tomato and the salt shaker.

It's not in season, the tomato, but the salt makes up for that.

Halfway through the last bite I cock my head back at the door, stare at it, finally nod to myself.

"I didn't order Chinese," I say at last, in my most normal voice.

Nobody knocks.

"Magazines again?" I add, as if into the other room.

Nothing.

Once I've caught the Number Ghosts this way. Scared them off anyway.

But not this time.

"Mary?" I finally try, not really loud enough for anybody. Unless she's already in my head.

Controlling my steps, making them so, so normal, I cross to the door, rattle the chain more than I need to in opening it, then just stand there.

Thin mints.

Three boxes, lined up like soldiers, like green and white bricks.

I swallow hard, look both ways—nothing, no one, empty— and try to taste the air. For one of Singer's lackeys, leaving me a message here, about a job not well done. For Dashboard Mary, leaving me another kind of message.

I can't taste anything, though.

Behind me, Kid Hoodie snickers.

I tighten my lips but don't turn around, don't give him that satisfaction.

And then a flutter down in the corner jerks my eyes over.

From baseboard to ceiling is the line of duct tape I finally had to press there two years ago and then iron flat, the iron shooting me with steam the whole time (that iron's gone now), the hot water scalding down the back of my hand (it runs different than blood), boiling the skin there (the least of my scars).

It was better than the alternative.

You'd think so too, had you been here then.

What had been happening was that that corner of the wallpaper, when the super had slopped it on twenty years ago, he hadn't used enough glue at the very bottom. What this meant was that over the years it had worked loose at the corner, enough to flutter a bit, exactly like a curtain, one trying to lift, to pull back. Starting to. In the worst way.

But now that duct tape, it's gone stiff, dried up.

And that coldness behind that wallpaper, that emptiness, that chasm, that yawning fucking gulf of blackness, I can feel it in my cheekbones again, so that my eyes are marbles, slick and alien in my head.

I close the door, set the chain, and the muscles in my hand are jerky, so that I have to use my other hand as a guide.

Kid Hoodie doesn't say anything about it.

He's learning.

So, two years ago.

Okay.

I got it into my head that the Chessire Arms wasn't the Chessire Arms at all.

The idea was that when Singer cracked the door of the storage unit that day, what he did was just study me for a long time. Like a bug, one nobody's seen for a long time. One everybody had kind of just thought was extinct. Except there I was, scuttling around on the concrete, sneering over my shoulder about this intrusion of light. This interruption.

In this version, he nurses Belinda back somehow. Halfway back, anyway. Maybe just a quarter, because everybody needs somebody who'll stay in one place like that. That they can go to and pet when they want. Her yoga helps the whole process—the kind of shape she was in already from it, I mean. It's what she did that whole first night, even, when I was trying to sleep, think of something good this time, not just put her through the same old paces.

But then it wormed its way into my head, the way she was breathing. The way she was controlling her breath.

Here she was, blood crusted on one side of her face already, one of her breasts cut into in a way she probably never planned—who

91

knows though, right?—one of her lips bitten through more or less, and she was shutting all that out. Just hitting pose after pose, position after position, stance after stance, whatever they're called. It made me think of people I've seen in the park before dawn, swimming through the dark like cartoon swans. Only, watching her, I got to thinking maybe it was only ever one person, and the rest were shadows, trying hard to do it good enough to be real.

It got to where my breathing started to synch up with hers, just because hers was making more sense. I was one of those shadows, at least in my head. On accident.

It's a bad line to step over, that one.

Well.

Unless you've still got the mettle to do what has to be done.

But she did try, I'll give her that. With just her eyes, when she was holding whatever stance. It's what finally made me put her tongue in that rubber, then take it out, use the rubber for its intended purpose, put the tongue back in, then use it again. I wanted her to shut up.

Her last words?

With her mouth, I mean, but with her eyes too I guess.

She saluted me. *Namaste.* And her voice wasn't flat or wavery or any of that. It was like she was talking to a part of me only she could see. A part she respected.

It's still the only time that's ever happened.

I stared at her a moment to be sure this wasn't a trick then nodded back to her, found myself watching the wall, still nodding, then settled back on her again, touched the brim of the hat I always mean to be wearing, and we got down to the dirty business at hand.

She came apart like a toy.

I remember every gristle, every pop, every last, accidental whimper—hers *and* mine.

But at the end of all that, sunlight pouring through the lifted door, making Singer and his goons fuzzy and bright like angels—

What if they were, kind of? Or had been.

It made as much sense as the other way, I mean. As much sense as Belinda being my job application.

The dog that chews up your kid, say, you don't take it home, buy it a little doggy bed and comb the knots out of its hair, do you?

No, what you do is you follow that dog into the alley with a shovel, then call it close with the mustardy last bite of a hamburger, and hit it right on the point of the hips first, where the spine bottlenecks. That way it can't run away. And then, man. Then you've got all night, brother. The rest of that particular dog's life.

It's what I would do.

Kid or no kid, yeah. Maybe the dog just looked at me wrong while I was driving by. Like it knew something. Could smell it on me.

But Singer. Singer had a *reason.*

What if he'd visited some of that kind of justice back onto me? What if he'd rolled that metal door down, pulled on a pair of long rubber gloves, and told his goons to watch and learn, boys.

Then what's this, then, the Chessire Arms?

This is why the duct tape in the corner. And the superglue rubbed down over it. All the blue marker crosses traced on top of that.

Vegetable Ghost, Number Ghost?

What if they're *all* ghosts, me included?

What if this is how it turns out in the end, that you have to live in a room with every last sap you ever did in? Only, individuals like myself, yeah. One room's not going to cut it, horsey boy. Not even one *house*. Try a run-down apartment building in the forgotten part of heaven. Everybody but me snickering behind their walls, about the big joke. Them all drawing straws to see who's coming to see me next, keep the joke going.

The shits.

All the same, though.

Say this is a joke, the Chessire Arms, the last joke. That what I'm grinding down the third sink is just being fed back through the faucet to me. That the kind of thing you really want to know? To have to know and then keep on living with?

So what you write on the supply list next door, what you write over and over in the most perfect letters, it's DUCT TAIP, DUCT TAIP, and then you stand there and close your eyes, listen for ghosts, laughing behind their hands.

It's no way to live.

After a while of that, you'll step outside the window one night between shows, just to prove to yourself that the concrete down there's really real.

It usually is.

If the thin mints are poison, then I'm immune, I guess. Unless it's a delayed thing.

I couldn't just let them sit there in the hall, though.

They were a little green and white beacon.

The ghosts across from me, who I only know from their footsteps—they could be goat-legged satyrs for all I know, ones that eat barbecued lamb chops every night then pick nits from each other's beards by television light—the next time they step out, they would see those three boxes.

The first packages ever left for me.

Their chance to finally introduce themselves?

Come on, dear. He's so quiet, he's got to be nice. Just put on your good—no, the other one. *And do your belt—*

This is how accidents happen.

There should be a series of public service announcements, really. Of Dick and Jane scooping up the unknown neighbor's cookies, skipping to the door then standing there with their hats in their hands, waiting to make nice.

And then, some boy peeking out his door down by the elevator, he sees it in silhouette: the bloody maw of this great chainsaw beast opening, sucking these two do-gooders down headfirst.

Or, better: stepping aside, ushering them in, then checking left and right down the hall, catching the drained-white boy's eye at the last possible instant, and smiling, winking.

The kind of wink that means later, yeah.

See you after dark, Scout.

Don't wait up.

And maybe that's what I should be doing, even. If nobody's coming to my door, I could put out a little bait.

Only, doing people too close to you, that can be bad news.

You have to range out. Do all different kinds.

I reel in the thin mints.

They taste like plastic, make me feel like an android.

Riley likes them, though.

I have to soak the two she gets in milk first, so she can get them down. With my hand on her forehead, no light at all, I can feel the muscles in her jaw, how they're pulling on her thin skull.

Thank you, I say to me, in her voice, in my head.

Because she would if she could.

I don't know what I'd do without her.

Kids, shit. They turn the best of us soft, I guess.

Later I do push ups to work the cookies off, and when my arms start to shake I do more, and more, biting fibers from the carpet on the way up, blowing them out on the way down.

I should have taken longer with the guy and the dog, I know now.

You've got to ration, got to make what you've got last.

Next time, though. Next time we'll go days, round and round. I'll be the carnie leaning down from the carousel, his smile painted on, his gloved hand reaching down.

Some rides never end.

I collapse into my chair, naked as the day—well, naked as a lot of the days, really.

When the sun comes, though, it's for me.

My pores open like mouths and drink the heat in and everything's perfect again.

It could be two weeks ago. The hours before Kid Hoodie slouched down my hall, his eyes in his hood like two dim lights, his mouth cutting this thin grin I already want to—

Shit.

What I'm staring at, just past the armrest, is the stupid little phone. The one I know inside-out, that I have no excuse not to be thumbing deeper into.

No excuse except that I don't want to know.

That it's easier not to.

But I'm not duct-taping over this, either.

I start doing that, and pretty soon the whole place'll be grey. My own padded room. Might as well just do my eyes and have it done with already.

No thanks.

I'm not stupid either, though.

To listen, I free up the wet-dry vac's cord, put my hand at the base of its spine like a cop and roll it into the living room with me, its little casters so eager.

Like they don't know the hall, the living room. Every little crack.

I check the front door once more, then end up checking the hall too—you never know—and touch the five usual things on the way back to my chair. Just another day.

"Well then," I say out loud, the father at dinner, in the moments after some domestic spat's just died down, and he's ready to go ahead and just eat the fucking meatloaf.

The phone's right there on top of its manual, just like it has been.

I palm it over, turn it up to face me, ready for the Dashboard Mary figurine to be there all holy and evil, but instead, now that the phone's got juice, and is connected, there's a message.

From—from when it was ringing before. Has to be. Because it hasn't rang since.

I stare at the notification like I can decipher it from arm's length, I guess. Scare it back deeper into the screen.

It's just a phone, though.

Nothing.

I nod to make this even more true and pull the manual over. Not for the directions to listen to the voice mail—I know that—but for the four numbers written down into the four boxes provided. Kid Hoodie's private code, for future reference. Should he get on a soap opera and catch amnesia or something.

Like it was meant to be, then—and what isn't, right?—I open right to that page. Probably because he had to cock it open to write in it. Cock it open far enough to break the spine over, so that the manual has a memory of him too.

I'll burn it later. Something special.

But now.

This has to be why Mary left it. If she left it on purpose, I mean, it was for this, so I could listen to the voice mail. I probably wasn't even supposed to find the voice memo, Kid Hoodie trying to . . . what? Protect himself by recording me?

Dumb shit.

What's that make me, though, yeah.

I didn't even know he had it. That phones could even do that.

Close. Too fucking close.

I blow air out my mouth long and slow, look far away, to a dozen other things I could be doing right this moment.

None of them are right.

And anyway, like my old man said once going into the office he'd just been fired from, a tire iron held low along his leg, me and my sister buckled into the backseat for the rest of the day: Better men than me have failed at lesser endeavors.

What he was talking about there was glory. How to get it, how to reach down into the world and rip it right the fuck out.

A voice mail, yeah.

Real scary.

I lean down, thumb one of the ear buds from the player into the phone's jack, then rotate my head, plug the other one in as well.

Like I already knew, it's Dashboard Mary. And she's in a car. I can tell, can hear it all around her, the space. Outside.

Someday I'm going to go to the roof, I know. Just to look around. To hold my hands out and turn in movie circles like I'm dancing with the air, with the whole world.

Right after I'm sure that I haven't been pulled up there on somebody else's strings, I mean. Right after I know there's not a police copter hovering just below the height of the building. The traffic copter from the news on the other side, some reporter in the field betting her career on commandeering this particular whirlybird, stacking cars up for miles in every direction.

I'll go outside right after I decide to be twelve years old again, I mean. And a girl.

Probably tomorrow, yeah.

Ha.

This is the first new message, from the first time the phone rang.

Dashboard Mary's whispering, covering the phone with her other hand, if I'm hearing right. But too, she's not even talking to Kid Hoodie: "I don't know why he's not responding, ma'am. This isn't like him at all. He's usually more—at least . . ."

And then it's over. Just that.

I don't smile. Don't know what to do.

The way she said *ma'am*, though.

I can feel the long muscles around my femur writhing. About to get into a tremble if I don't hold them down.

She was talking to somebody older, was the thing. And there was apology in her voice. But a kind of apology she's practiced at too. A kind she's tired of already. That's become routine.

I push all the buttons I can, pull the phone away, drag the wires down. Stand up, walk all around the room, careful never to step over the wet-dry vac's cord.

It leaves me walking every part of a circle around the couch but the most important part.

Ma'am.

I'm not crying either. Guys like me don't, not from something like this.

Ma'am. Mam. Mom.

She was talking to a mom is what she was doing.

Without even having to think about it, I run to the trap door, kick it open like it's counterbalanced for but then have to go back to the living room, lay flat-ass on the floor to go *under* the cord, complete the circle. No clue why I didn't think of that first.

I nod that that's done then, don't let myself look to the kitchen, to Kid Hoodie, because I know what it's going to look like over there: not a medical school skull with clay on it, a cut-off sweatshirt draped over, but Kid Hoodie himself, standing up from behind the counter but standing very still, like I won't see him.

And I'm *not* breathing as hard as it sounds like, all raspy and deep.

And I'm not running to her.

Except that I am.

"I'm sorry," I say, and instead of opening the trapdoor the rest of the way, to crash through, make my escape or die trying,

I let it down just enough that the counterweight touches her head against the ceiling below me. And then I'm up again, in the bathroom, pulling the medicine cabinet door off its rusted hinges so I can hold it down through the crack in the floor, see her upside down, glass bottles hanging from all her fingers like she's forever falling through space: Mom.

I lower my face to the bunched-up carpet.

The fibers stick to my cheeks and to the snot from my nose.

"You're still here," I whisper, because she is.

She's not the ma'am Dashboard Mary was talking to. Not the mom. She couldn't be. I don't know what I was thinking.

Stupid stupid stupid.

But still.

As punishment, so I'll learn, I make myself listen to the next voice message before I'm ready.

It's still her, Dashboard Mary.

She's humming to herself. The kind of humming you do while you're working, I think. Doing a thing you've done day-after-day for the last twenty weeks, as far as you can remember back. Anybody who's ever pushed a mop knows.

It's not even a song, either, really. Or—no, it is.

Come and knock on my door. Just the tune.

God.

That's why Kid Hoodie made it her ringtone.

Or maybe she did it one night while he was in the other room. As a surprise.

"Now just," Mary says then, nearly two weeks ago, the *just* almost strained, like she's . . . lifting something? "All better," she says when it's over. "Now just—" and then time's up, the message is over.

I swallow hard, almost lose it.

For a long time it's just my face in my hands.

Nothing creaks. Not caster wheels, not the clay to either side of Kid Hoodie's mouth. There's just the empty hum from the phone. It fills my head, cuts my tether for a bit so that I'm floating all around.

That's why I was thinking Mom. It's the way Dashboard Mary was talking. That tone. *All better.* It's what they say to their kid, leaning over him in bed, and then they pat it down so it'll stick, their kisses, and the number of times they tap, it's the magic number. The number that keeps the kid's soul from getting taken in the night, or whatever the rhyme was.

But. Too.

That's also how nurses talk to their patients, isn't it?

The sheet-changing nurses, keeping their ward of grown-men babies happy and alive, their souls folded into their chests like sleeping birds.

I bite both my cheeks at once, shake my head no, no.

There's no blood, though. And I'm biting hard enough to bite through, right? Shit shit shit.

I open my mouth, suck both cheeks in, and slam the heel of my hand up against my chin so that the black in my eyelids fizzes, burns like the coldest star.

Then the blood comes.

I make myself swallow it all, and feel on the outside of my face, for teeth pushing through. There's just heat. No white.

No *nurse* white.

I laugh at how stupid I'm being. This is starting to be like the old days, some motel manager knocking on the door like he's down a tunnel a thousand miles long. A whole host of interesting things in the bottom of the ice machine down the hall, that they won't find for weeks.

Nurse Mary.

Yeah.

What would a nurse be doing with a nothing like Kid Hoodie? A punk like Jason Pease? She'd have at least gotten him off cigarettes. Kept him out of Trouble.

It's bullshit, whatever I was hearing. Has to be.

To prove it, I play it again and again and again. Smooth the carpet back over the trapdoor, the palms of my hands inches away from the soles of her feet. The mannequin's.

This is what it was, what I heard: Dashboard Mary was down in the car—no, that second call was a day later. She was back, was trolling around the Chessire Arms, and finally parked all illegal somewhere. Because that's the only kind around here. So she had to be on constant lookout. Any girlfriend of Kid Hoodie would know that the law's bad news.

And of course she brought food. This was a stakeout.

And of course she called him once, but made herself hang up before it started ringing. Before she thought it started ringing. But the call went long enough for Kid Hoodie's voice mail to pick up, to record what she was doing: smoothing out a sandwich wrapper on the seat. While trying to balance her drink between her legs. Smoothing out her wrapper and balancing the drink and talking to herself because she was alone. Everybody does it: *There, there, all better.*

If you're alone too much, you can hear anything in anything. Because there's no one to tell you otherwise, just yourself. And nobody's their own monitor.

It's why going to your room for a day or two when you're a kid, to think about what you've done, it's the worst.

But I'll be damned if Singer's going to do that to me.

The phone's charged now. I could call her if I wanted. Ask her to bring me a sandwich too, then very carefully, very intentionally, so that she'll have to hear, flatten the paper out on the couch beside me until each crinkle's gone. So that she can't help but knowing that I've heard her when she thought she was alone. That I've been there beside her.

And maybe it's better this way. The cat and mouse.

So long as we each remember who's who.

I hiss a laugh out, and it hardly even sounds that fake.

Because I can, to show that I can, I play the voice mail another time, and another, then rip the ear buds down to plug them into Kid Hoodie, let him hear what he can't have anymore, but then stuff them back into my ears to try to catch what she's whispering to him.

She knows it's me again, is already saying the same thing over.

I'm not stupid, though.

I plug one into Kid Hoodie, one into me, but then get the clay in my ear like warm spit and just sling the whole fucking contraption across the room, scream after it to keep it away.

It bolos around the oak coat rack with the brass hooks, finally winds down, too tangled for anything.

But I can still hear something. Kid Hoodie's stupid drum music, thumping in my head like it's infected me. I shake my head no, step across the room to grind the thing under my foot, but—

That's not what I'm hearing, music.

What I'm hearing's just *after* the thump, the bump, the beat. Like an echo, just without sound. Like the shape the sound was, half a moment ago.

And then I stand fast, know what that shape was: a hand, balled into a fist. The door. Somebody knocking.

I push across the room not touching anything, fling the door open.

Nothing, no one.

I nod about this like it's right, it's expected, then latch onto the jamb, lean out, look down to the right.

Framed against the metal of the elevator door there just for a moment is a stoop-shouldered shape in some bullshit light green jumpsuit, I guess. Turning right into the stairway. Leaned over like he's running away, except he's walking even slower than usual. Singer's sending me the senior citizens now, walkers and all.

I hiss, almost step out, almost give chase, just do him in the stairwell, drive the side of his head into the corner of the wooden banister until the thin bone there eggshells opens, strings the bloody yolk between my fingers.

But I don't.

Leave those kinds of theatrics for the short-timers.

And I'm already laughing some anyway.

I close the door, hold it shut, and know that if I turn around at the wrong moment, what I'm going to see's Kid Hoodie's head, balanced on top of the wet-dry vac.

I never should have turned my back. Probably exactly what she wanted.

At the same time it scares me a little, that I'm not worried about Green Leisure Suit getting away. Or, no, that's not right: Green *Paper* Suit. Green Paper Suit Man.

Because that's what it was. One match and he's gone.

Except it wasn't a suit either.

I pull my ground-meat inner cheeks between my teeth again. Scrubs.

He was wearing scrubs.

Leaning forward because he was pushing a stainless steel cart of some kind. And not even looking back at me.

And maybe I do cry a little then, but I finally luck onto a place above my knee I can bite down onto, hold myself in place.

It's not great, not even close to perfect, but it's enough. My other hand holding the corner of the wallpaper down.

106

There are days like these, too.

Some amount of time later, I don't know, I'm in the kitchen. Because I have to, because it's come to this, I'm wearing the cut-in-half wet-dry vac tube on my arms like sleeves, a shoestring running behind my neck to keep them on. It turns me into a robot, and robots aren't pussies, don't have to think what they don't want to think.

I could never go through the trapdoor like this. I can't even walk over it because she'll know. They all will down there, are probably already making eyes at each other, worried. But I can make up for it. By not answering the phone when it rings.

I don't go to the window, don't answer the phone.

What I do instead is eat so much overcooked eggplant with mustard that I throw some of it back up, and stare at it there on my plate, just chewed, hardly digested, cheek blood threaded in and out like a tapeworm.

Because I'm nice, I collect it in five spoons, balance them all the way next door, and feed Riley.

She moans, shudders, finally opens her mouth for more, like a baby bird.

I don't watch any television for the next twenty-four hours.

The phone rings two more times but cuts off on the third ring. Halfway through it, each time.

Kid Hoodie looks over from his corner under the table, wants so bad to answer.

All the more reason not to.

I know what I want to tell her, though. I want to sit on the floor by the coat rack with that tangled-up phone pressed to the side of my head and tell her that I figured it out. That I didn't even have to leave my apartment either, do what I was thinking over and over: go door-to-door all up and down the hall, seeing if the Green Paper Clothes Man, the *real* nurse, if he had a reason to be on this floor or not.

Not that I would have minded.

All it would take is some polite knocking. I'm the guy who lives a few doors down, yeah, that one, hey. What? Oh, just wondering any of a hundred things, whatever gets me in the door, lets me see if there's any bedbound renters here. Anybody in need of a house call.

If not, great.

Then just move from room to room, push something (my thumbs, with the metal thimbles sharp on the end) into the eyes of everybody who had the bad luck to see me. And everybody else besides, just stack them up like wood in the lefthand apartment, everybody *including* the geezer with the bedsores and the catheter, who would probably lift his face to help me get the angle right. Because he's ready, has been ready for years.

Nevermind that I love him, or would, if I'd had to actually go down there.

But he's there all the same.

It's the only explanation.

Otherwise, Mary Dear, I have to believe that you staged those calls, planted that guy in the hall, and that Girl Scout in her green uniform before him, just to get my eyes used to the color. That you know about me. That you razored some pages out of that manual, that that little phone has some function where you can call without ringing and then just listen in.

And I should have answered the door sooner yesterday, I know that too.

Then Green Paper Clothes Man, he could have just told me all this. All about you.

But I know anyway.

So send that cute little Girl Scout back if you want, sure.

I never did earn my dissection patch.

I'm not supposed to, and don't have any money for it, and it's just going to draw attention, and it'll leave Chessire Arms there in the call log, but still. If Singer's not going to feed me, I'm going to have to feed myself.

I lower myself to the tangled-up phone, raise it to the side of my head—latex glove on now, of course—and dial in the number from the magnet on the refrigerator.

Pizza, yeah.

The kid who answers has to say the name of the place three times (I add twice more in my head) before I manage to get anything out: "Cheese."

I'm the troll under the bridge, mumbling up at the people walking in the bright sunshine.

He doesn't hear me, is already reading some spiel off. Wings, buy a medium get a large, I don't know.

"No meat," I cut in, louder now, and just let it hang there.

I'm not wearing the wet-dry vac sleeves anymore either. They're duct-taped back into a single tube, are back where they're supposed to be.

And it's not like I've never done this before. Ordered a pizza boy.

Before, though—two times, in different states, different

outfits, different types of pizza in different sizes—I always had the hundred dollar bill there on the table for when the doorbell rang.

Trick is, when the pizza boy has to start thinking about taking that hundred, about what not having change is going to do for his next three deliveries, you can use it. Take the hundred back and ask if a twenty'd be better?

It always is. Especially for a twelve-dollar pizza. That usually means the pig ordering it'll just take the five back, wave the three away, thanks, kid.

But that twenty, man, it's always buried in some pants in the laundry way back in the motel's bathroom, you think.

And everybody knows the doors on those rooms lock.

Like that, he's in, nevermind his training, all the horror stories.

I'm just a guy on the road. A three-dollar tipper, maybe.

Who'm I going to tell anyway, right?

Yes, manager sir, your delivery boy did actually step into the room to keep the door from closing, to keep himself from having to knock again like a fool, maybe losing that third dollar.

I was so shocked, so insulted, so terrified. What would Mrs. Pig back in Wisconsin think? That I do this on every trip, invite young boys into my room late at night?

Yeah.

So maybe I do.

But not for what you think.

These days, though, I've been burning all the paper money in the oven, flushing it.

The position it puts me in is that, first, I don't have any real ruse to get the kid in here, and, second, if the hall's full of some police parade that just happens to be going by, it won't matter. I'll still be committed to grabbing the pizza boy by the back of the neck, pulling him into what the news will probably call my lair.

But I can't let him walk, either. He'll have seen me. Have knocked on my door. Even if I'm just that prick who wanted company, a snapshot of something young to jack off to later, that dillhole who pretended to not have ordered that boring ass pie, still, I'll be *some*body to him.

As soon as that happens, it's like you're already writing your own suicide letter.

All it takes is some slow old detective to happen to talk to the wrong person at the wrong time, to file whatever they say into the same place as something three other people said two years ago that didn't mean a damn thing either, and then, before you know, that greydick's waking up at three in the morning, suddenly knows everything about you.

"*He's the cheese pizza guy,*" he'll say to his wife, snapping his fingers in the dark. "*Give me the phone, Gretchen.*"

No thanks.

I like the name, though: Gretchen.

She sounds like she'd be limber, maybe, but watch you in a kind of haunted way when you don't think you know she can see you from the other room.

Yeah.

"Sir?" the kid on the end of the phone's saying now. "Mr., um, Mr. Pease?"

My heart stops beating. Beats backwards. Dies.

I bark out a little sound, twist the phone away from my mouth, the shapes my lips are trying not to make.

Kid Hoodie's watching me from his sideways place under the table.

I look away slowly, have both hands on the phone now to talk.

"Do you want it delivered to the front desk again?" the kid says.

"Front desk," I repeat. The words are just sounds.

"You have to leave the money with the girl, though. My guy can't wait for them to page you again, okay?"

I laugh a little. Through my eyes, it feels like.

It hurts.

I focus instead on the idea of everybody on the floor stacked against the wall in the lefthand apartment. On if I really *had* sharp thimbles like that, to push through eyes. How I'd probably have to fit garden hose gaskets over my thumbs, to keep the thimbles from filling with eye yolk.

But don't thimbles have holes, too, for gription?

"Front desk," I say again, almost calmer.

"If you had an office . . ." the kid leads off, like I'm supposed to finish.

"Front desk," I tell him.

It's starting to mean something.

That I *don't*. Have an office. That, I don't know. That my desk, the one I work at, the one Jason Kid Hoodie Pease works at, that he used to work at when he worked, it's not in an office with walls and a window or two. It's just out in the middle of everything, with everybody else. In the soup with the rest of the suits.

I want to hold the phone over to him, let him finish the order, but I don't know what he'd say either. That glint in his eye.

Yeah, trust him.

"Okay then," the kid at the pizza place says, doing something else at the same time it sounds like, "that'll be, with tax, and including the newspaper discount, eleven-seventy-nine."

He closes by saying they've got a cheese coming out of the oven right now. That it'll be about twenty minutes. And to leave the money with the girl.

I nod thanks, find the red button, hold it down like it might all be about to get away from me.

"No," I say out loud, shaking my head to make it true. "*No.*"

But then I thumb through Kid Hoodie's contacts.

Before I can talk myself out of it, I highlight WORK, swallow so that it's loud in my ears. Call.

The girl who answers halfway through the first ring, which is days and weeks and lifetimes before I'm ready, what she says in her chipper, ready-to-help voice, it's the name of the newspaper.

Then, "Hello? Hello?"

I shake my head no, nothing.

Please.

When I choke the Vegetable Ghost with the charger cord of the phone the next morning, it's nothing personal. It's like I heard a guy on television explain masturbation once: it's mowing the lawn, pretty much. Not what you really want to do, and your shoes are green and nasty afterwards, but still, here you are. Somebody had to do it, right?

Because I know now that he might be my one drink of water in the desert, I spend most of the morning with my knee in his back, between his shoulder blades, the charger cord looped around my hands, making the piano wire cuts bleed. In the good way.

The Vegetable Ghost cries and pisses and shits and throws up and runs red from the nose and from the eyes, but I shake him back to me each time, for another round.

It's bullshit, though.

It's not at all the same as having somebody knock on your door, a hesitant look in their eyes, like maybe they're in the wrong place.

They are.

And the thing is, the Vegetable Ghost knew it, had known it for the last two weeks already.

Me doing this to him, it's just what he's been expecting.

It's so fake, so forced, that I almost even let him go, lesson learned, sorry, bub, no hard feelings, ha, but then when he wakes up the next time he's not all there anymore.

As an experiment, I take some of the copper tubing from the dishwasher (who's going to use it anymore, right?), run it up the Vegetable Ghost's nose until it mushes into brain, and then—it's CPR—I blow gently, trying to give him the oxygen I'd evidently cut off for ten or twenty seconds too long.

It doesn't work, even when I breathe in deep, blow into his head with everything I have. All that happens is that his tear ducts burble their sad little burbles.

This isn't usually how it goes, no.

I mean, sure, sometimes they'll konk before you're all-the-way done with them, but that's live and learn. Next time you'll know not to push so far so fast.

I shrug, tap the end of the copper straw, and stand away from the Vegetable Ghost.

For a long time I try to think of what to write on the list, finally just come up with the usual produce, but then laugh.

Who's going to take the list today?

It's funny.

I turn to see if the Vegetable Ghost gets it, but there's pinkish grey bubbling up from his straw.

The look on his face, though, it's so serene.

"You're welcome," I tell him, and squat down, swirl the straw around some then cap the end with my index finger, pop it out all at once, turning it upside down fast.

What I was thinking about was blowing it all in some mean-ingful pattern on the wallpaper. Some intentional, meaningless splatter for the next Ghost to study.

But I don't.

The brain plops and gulps out the bottom of the straw. Twelve years of math and science and english and cheerleader fantasies, drip-dripping away.

I step back so it won't get on the toe of my shoe. But it doesn't really matter either.

The Dead Vegetable, his left leg jerks a bit, rattles around like he's trying to shake one last thing from his pants leg, and then he's still.

I go through the barrel he brought, shelf all the produce, don't touch the hackysack at the bottom that I'm sure I wouldn't have asked for, that has to be some sort of setup, then get the rod from the front closet, sit the Vegetable Ghost up onto the barrel.

"Any last words?" I say to him.

My hand's kind of pushing through a hole in his back now, around the warm column of his spine, my fingers as far into his mouth as I can get them, from the back.

It doesn't work as well as I thought. It's just more bullshit.

I shake my head, tell him it's not his fault, and plant the butt of another closet rod just below his bellybutton, start pushing him down into the barrel ass-first.

It's hard because usually I grind them down in my kitchen first.

It's hard because I never put them in the barrels at all.

But today is a new day.

I pretend the barrel's the end of that great wet-dry vac in the sky, just doing what it does.

When he's in enough I tamp the lid down the plastic wrap around the edges. Because who knows when his replacement'll come to dolly him away.

To show I'm not such a bad guy, I go ahead and tip the barrel up onto the dolly, angle it towards the front door.

On the white board, too, as a joke nobody's supposed to get but me, I write *thinmints* real small down in the corner, then smile my way back next door.

The next morning is better. Maybe the Vegetable Ghost was good for me after all.

The sun when it comes is a blessing, is just what I need.

Minutes after it's gone, the oil I've got on is still warm from it.

Kid Hoodie doesn't say anything, and I just let him look all he wants. Soak me in like I've been soaking in the light.

This time when the phone rings its five full times, I don't even open my eyes.

Just another thing. Something I can whir dead in any disposal I choose. My—yeah. It's *my* copper straw, the one connecting me to the outside world.

I've seen how that can work, though. How it can not work.

That was probably even the lesson I was teaching myself, without knowing it.

My copper tube, Kid Hoodie's phone, the only one I've ever kept—none of the others ever played the Jack Tripper song, so it's not really my fault—it's the thing that can either save me or kill me. And most likely the second of those. Exhibit number one: a certain pizza operator having that phone number already in his system.

But that was a blessing too, of sorts.

If it hadn't been in the system, then I would have had to give him this address, or try to make one up.

And I would have never known about the newspaper.

Kid Hoodie wasn't recording us playing Trouble to use it to keep himself alive. He was recording us playing Trouble as part of a story.

And yeah, it could be a story on any of a hundred things: the short life and rough times of the workaday undercover agent; what it's like to be part of this idiot wave of youth; how to be a thug, the underbelly of the city, what happens when the lights go off, and on and on. He might have even been using his pen and notebook to investigate Singer. And then he either somehow really made it to me, or Singer got wise to him, told him he liked him, yeah, but first, there's this one guy he needed to see, see?

Except I know it wasn't any of that.

He was writing about *me*.

And what this means. What this has to mean.

Every time I think about it I have to make a fist from my hand, hold it sideways, breathe slow through it.

He was writing about me.

I've become enough of what people talk about on the streets that it's percolated all the way up to the newspaper. Or the step before the newspaper anyway. The step where this young reporter trades it all in for an ounce of proof. Because even an ounce, a whisper, a recording of a voice making small talk over a board game, it'll be enough.

What that says is that—what that says is that what they're saying about me, that there's this boogeyman living on the fortieth floor of some skyscraper, eating anybody who comes to his door (never), that the legend's big enough and heavy enough and wild enough that just a drop of truth is enough to make the whole thing true. Like if you believe in angels, then find this white feather in the alley, then those angels are all real now.

Or devils, so that you comb up goat hair from your grass one morning, save it in a baggie when nobody's looking.

Kid Hoodie was here for me.

It wasn't murder, what I did to him. It was self-defense.

And way too fast for someone like him.

And to think I ate cereal with him. Trusted him to watch for robot arms in the hall while I slept, sure that the place was safe for the night.

I should have killed him twice. Three times. Fifty.

And it's not over yet either. Won't be until Dashboard Mary's here too. Because you don't go into a thing like this alone. Your girlfriend, you tell her at least.

Just keep the car right around the building somewhere, yeah. And if I'm not back in twenty minutes, then call, I'll say I've got to—yeah, a family thing, like last time. That'll work. He won't be able to hear. I know, shit yeah. You're a doll. I love you. I love you love you love you thank you I'll be right back promise promise okay one more no no don't I've got to it's okay I'll be I love you bye.

He should have never walked away from that car.

He should have never looked up into the sky, along the side of some tall building, and thought I might be up there.

I am.

As far as Riley knows, this is what happened, what's *happening*: the day she walked into my apartment, her dad really was in the other room. Deal was, he was hiding. The bad guys all knew his name somehow. His good friend, me, an ex-cop myself, was giving him a place to crash. Not even his wife could know. It was better that way. Safer.

Except then, when Riley was crossing the linoleum I had unrolled across the dining room back then, one of the bad guys had somehow spidered into the apartment.

Because he knew better than to try to go into the living room, face her dad and his detective gun that never missed, he crept up behind her, did what he did to the back of her head, and then, when I was suddenly there trying to protect her, to cover her little body with my own, the bad guy did the same blurry thing to me. Only I was older, so died right there.

It was all pretty heroic.

Girls like that kind of stuff.

After that, her dad ran in to see what all the sound was about and his world kind of ended: there was his little girl on the floor, bleeding. His best friend in the world dead beside her. A skinny shadow of a bad guy flitting out of the room, gibbering, maybe even wearing a jester hat.

Good old Detective Dad did the only thing he could. He hammered boards over all the doors and windows. And the whole time he was doing that, he could hear the bad guys on the other side of the doors and windows, hammering their own boards on, and then iron bars on top of that, and then cement after that.

If they couldn't kill me (the dad), then they could bury me.

The coward's way, yeah.

But I didn't make detective at thirty-four for nothing.

Before they could know what was happening, I tunneled next door, tunneled to every apartment on this floor, and came back with an armful of food each trip. And I could have stayed gone any one of those times, but, really, I couldn't: you were here, Riley. I could never leave you.

So, by the time the bad guys figured out what I was doing and boarded and barred and cemented over the second apartment, I had enough food for a few years, if we rationed it, if we ate just enough to keep us alive. But there could be no light. We'd have to move like shadows, and always whisper, and stay very very still all the time. Our one break, too, was the water. The bad guys could turn it off, sure, thirst us out, dry us up, but I think they know that I could just break into the wall if I wanted, crack open a pipe. Sure, it'd make a mess, but when whoever's ceiling got wet called the super, then the jig would be up.

What's with this cement, Dan? You remember the fourth floor having a bomb shelter? Maybe we better call the city, see about load bearing fire hazard blah blah nothing.

So what we do in this measured truce, this waiting time, is live like mice. Like father and daughter mice, the father scurrying in to the second apartment as often as he can to feed the daughter, but trying hard to maintain a normal profile next door too, in the lighted apartment. Watching television, doing dishes for one, vacuuming at all hours. In case they've drilled a camera in like they probably have, to keep an eye on me.

You can't be too careful, I mean.

And as for that friend who traded it all in to protect this dad, who died trying to save the daughter, Billy was his name, and he's memorialized now in three rolls of plastic in the closet, standing up. Billy who gave his life for you.

And as for me, Riley, I could have left any day, but I never will.

This is a dream, really.

Now I don't have to worry about you sneaking out at night, I don't have to worry about boys knocking on the door. I don't have to worry about you leaving lights on or dropping glasses in the kitchen or getting braces or ever saying you hate me or anything. I can just straighten your hair down along the bed and whisper into your ear about how it's all going to be all right. How it's all going to be even more all right. Soon they'll forget about me, and the concrete around the apartments will crack open like an egg, release us out into the sunlit world like two butterflies.

Until then, though, we're caterpillars, eating whatever mash I can make from our limited supplies. Giving you most of it, the best of it.

This is what daddies do, dear.

This is the way we are.

The only hard part, really, is remembering to duck into the detective shield each time I cross over into the righthand apartment. Because she can see it glinting around my neck, I think.

It makes her eyes shiny and happy, sometimes even makes the outside fingers of her right hand tremble and reach.

What I do then is I take her hand in mine, guide it to the shield. Hold it there until she falls asleep again.

She can't see my eyes, I'm pretty sure.

That's probably for the best.

Because I'm nobody's puppet, I clean the bloody charger cord with five squares of toilet paper and get the cell phone out of the microwave.

It's already blinking about a new voice mail before I even give it the juice, but I don't want it stuttering halfway through, maybe erasing something vital.

Maybe Mary's calling to thank me for the pizza. If she's the girl at the front desk of the newspaper offices. But she'd have had to pay for it too. Somebody would have.

I don't know.

Last night I took the wet-dry vac apart again, just usual maintenance. The whole thing disassembled there on the carpet, the television light flickering over it.

I don't have to put it back together each time. I put it back together because I want to.

But this time. It's like a joke.

This time, all the usual parts in their usual places, wiped down with alcohol pads and then a light solution of bleach, there was still a rattle from the canister.

It made me think of roulette, and thinking of roulette made me push away fast, all the way to the wall.

The sound of roulette is the sound of a marble.

Sure enough.

With another closet rod I tipped the canister over, apologizing the whole time for the disrespect, then tapped on the undercarriage until the world had to show itself a little.

A single cat-eye marble, flashing down into the carpet.

Staring at me.

I shrugged, looked around, Kid Hoodie snickering under his table, then reached down, touched the carpet in front of the marble with the middle finger of my right hand then with my index finger, then with my ring finger, galloping so that I cycle all at once to five, in a perfect swirl the world can't counter, and wind up back in the middle.

And then I take it, swallow it.

It's a pearl now. It's mine. All it can see is me.

It's made me stronger, I mean.

Strong enough that I don't even have to go to the blinking voice mail first. That would be doing what she wants.

I might as well just start answering when it rings, then.

Maybe I should start calling in tips on myself, even.

Word is there's this guy, see, he's up in a—you've heard of him? Yeah, well, know where he lives?

They'd line up at my door, stack up in the lefthand apartment. Head-to-toe, I mean. I'd give them the real scoop, yeah. The down and dirty, the inside story.

But it would cost them.

Everything.

That's probably what she wants me to do, though. What she's goading me towards. The happy ending for her, for what I did to Kid Hoodie, is for me to be out in the street, blood steaming off one of my arms, a hostage under the other arm, spotlights baking thousands of kilowatts into my skin, my chest dancing with little red bugs.

She'd be there then, I know. Just watching the show. Eating a piece of cheese pizza, maybe, like everything's right in her world now.

But no.

It'd be a meat lover's pizza.

She's not like me, I mean.

Nobody is.

And the way I know that's what she wants is that, right now, wherever she is, she knows that her boyfriend's not coming back. And she knows the door to my apartment, whatever number's on it today.

Instead of calling the law, though, she's trying to handle this one herself.

Because it's personal to her.

Her first mistake.

If it ever gets personal, then you can't tell when to step away. You're always thinking just a little more time, that you can stay in this for a minute or two longer, nothing bad's going to happen, it's all going to work out.

It's not personal to me, though, babe.

You'll wish you'd known that earlier, trust me.

Look away even for a moment and I'll take you by the chin, wrench your face around, make you see the way the world really is. The way I see it.

Like I'm even going to listen to any of her voice mail bullshit.

Let other people play games. What I do, it's dead serious.

I go back to the voice memos. For nostalgia. To hear Kid Hoodie, when he thought he was going to live forever.

It makes me hard on accident.

I look over to him under the table and smile my best leery smile, put my hand in my pants some.

It's one thing I've never tried, getting off to the voice of the recently departed while that recently departed watches.

I hit play again, again, until it's a frenzy, until I'm almost there, but then stab down too deep into the button, access some older voice memo but pause it just as fast.

I pull my hand up, cradle the little phone.

The date is weeks before he ever came to see me.

Weeks.

It's a note, from Kid Hoodie to himself. The way reporters do, I guess.

Just this, whispered while he's walking in some crowded place: "She says a nurse."

She says a nurse.

I'm not hard anymore.

I can feel the marble growing in me, now.

What'll happen is that I'll open my eyes in my bed one night, and my irises'll flicker and waver, stand up into the blue cat-eye flame.

And then I don't know who I might be.

But I can't cut it out of my gut, either.

I sit on the counter, lean on the refrigerator. Stare across the dining room table.

A nurse, she said.

This is what she wants me to think: that the Chessire Arms isn't an apartment building at all. That it's Chessire Arms Mental Facilities. Chessire Arms Asylum. Chessire Arms Home for the Criminally Insane.

That—that it's not a place I came to voluntarily. That my apartment, it's just the one assigned to me, and that I've wrapped up so deep inside myself that all I can hear is snatches of her conversation filtering down.

To my mother, coming on a Sunday to visit: *I don't know why he's not responding.*

To me, when I'm conked: *there there, all better.*

She doesn't want to kill me, to do to me some version of what I did to Kid Hoodie. That's not it at all.

She either wants to pull back the curtain, show me who I really am, make me acknowledge it, or she wants to trick me into thinking that's who I really am. That I maybe killed somebody once in a motel room, sure. Maybe even a couple one week. But that I got locked up for that, started hiding inside my head, where the spree could go epic. Never have to stop.

Could there really be somebody like me? Living in a room where the punks just come knocking?

I wouldn't buy it. If I can't, though, the next question's worse: Do they wheel me around, or just leave me in my room?

Whatever she wants, I suppose.

Whatever she wants me to think.

And the only way I can prove her wrong, or right, is to leave. To go down to the street, be sure it's the street, not just more mental real estate. See whether that was me wearing scrubs the other day. Walking away from myself.

But that can't be.

I remember it all so well, the shit I've done. The taste, the grit, the shudders. The way that, even if you take a voice box apart and blow gently across the little curtains of muscle, that still, you can't make it make the meaty sound you want.

And I knew it was wrong when I was doing it, even. I just did it anyway. But I wouldn't know it was wrong if I had gone off the deep end, would I? The wrong of it's half the fun.

And—and I'm careful each time, anyway. Too careful, smarter than I need to be. They never would have caught me, would they?

Until Belinda, yeah. The unnatural brunette. Downward Facing Dog Woman.

I laugh a bit, so that my shoulders shake with it.

It's so fake.

Says a kid on visiting day, tugging his mom's sleeve: "Who's that guy over there in his chair, crying?"

He's not crying, honey. Don't stare. That's a chuckle, see? He's probably thinking about something good, from before.

That's not me.

I don't care what she says.

But.

She says a nurse.

I close my eyes as tight as I can, push the heels of my hands over them too.

This means they had me, the story of me, in their sights for months already. They had time, time to—

She says a nurse.

She says that a nurse. She says that a nurse would . . . what? Work?

That has to be what Kid Hoodie meant, talking to himself as he walked through whatever lobby.

That a nurse would work on me.

That that's the kind of trick that would give them the advantage they needed. The kind that would reduce me not just to their level, but to lying there in a bed all day, staring, the past not the past anymore, but a stolen thing. Something ripped away from me. Along with everything that *is* me.

It's not about Kid Hoodie for her. Kid Hoodie was just collateral damage, a pawn she had to sacrifice to get in my head, a human bridge between us.

It was never about the story for her, never about going public. That's just what she told Kid Hoodie, when she found him wherever she found him, and got him to believe that something like this could make his career, make him famous.

Word about me isn't on the streets at all.

Singer'd never let that happen.

But she knew. She knows.

I've been what she's after the whole time.

Revenge.

Unless her shift goes over at eleven, yeah. Unless she has a closet full of sterile white hose.

Shit.

I pull my hands down my face, lean forward to a sound not like casters.

It's drier, somehow.

Fingertips, reaching up around the corner edge of the wallpaper by the door. Nails not painted at all, the skin bloodless.

I breathe in sharp, plant my hand behind me to keep from falling, and hit the disposal switch. The whole countertop shakes under me.

I grub back, turn it off, my eyes only leaving the corner by the door for a flash.

It's enough.

The hand's gone.

This time I pack the wallpaper down with molding clay, and then spray lighter fluid on it, and then light it, cook it into a doughy stone.

As punishment, I breathe in as much of the green smoke as my lungs'll let, and then when the smoke alarm in the hall starts to scream I pull the door open before I can remember not to.

There's the sound of footsteps in both directions, people rushing around, I don't know.

Just the sound, though. Because I'm not looking.

All I can see is the square package I'm standing over.

I turn my head to the side and grab it with both hands, slide it in. Pour a whole pitcher of lemonade over the smoldering clay. Slide the chain on the door back and forth, back and forth, waiting for the footsteps outside to die down.

They finally do.

From the window I watch the rest of the drama: a fireman talking to a mom, the mom's fingers clamped onto the upper arm of some skater punk.

What they do is take his cigarettes out. The fireman grinds the whole pack between his gloved fingers, then kisses the flakes away.

After that I draw the curtain.

They're not coming up here.

That's all that matters.

That and the package.

It's from nobody, to nobody.

But I know.

I balance it on the middle rack of the oven and open it with tongs and a coat hanger.

It's a Girl Scout uniform. *The* Girl Scout uniform.

Her name was Alissa.

I leave it in the oven.

In a haze the next morning, trying to blink away the sunlight I usually just drink, I make my way through the short door and into the lefthand apartment.

As for any dreams I might have had, they were from the marble swimming through my veins, so hardly count.

What I'm wearing doesn't matter. Some old slacks, no shirt, two-day socks.

The reason it doesn't matter—I only remember as I'm letting a quick five flutter on the wall outside the closet I duck through, the wall I have to use to pull myself forward into the lefthand apartment—is that there isn't a Vegetable Ghost. Or, there is, but he's tamped down into a barrel assfirst, the way you'd store a doll, maybe. If you really wanted to just be throwing it away.

And there's no smell, because of the plastic wrap on the barrel.

Some grey matter on the floor, sure, but brains don't ever smell like real meat. The bugs'll get into them, but they're not particular either, can't be trusted. The thing with brains probably has something to do with what they say about each animal having just enough to tan their own hide. I don't know, haven't tried that one yet.

But it's not just brains, either. You have to pee into that mix too. Some right amount.

It's not the best day so far, I mean.

I lean back, arc a line of bright yellow down onto the grey stain on the carpet, and am just getting worried about it mixing somehow with the other pee on the floor—I don't want to be like them—when a flashbulb pops all around me and time slams to a stop long enough for me to appreciate steam rising suddenly from my line of pee, exactly like the pee's breathing out, relaxing. Or like it's a warm river in the early morning, the fog clinging to it, riding it.

Then things start moving again.

I'm arching my back as far forward as I can, as far as anybody ever has.

No time to scream yet, but it's coming.

There's somebody behind me, with something dull and hot.

A cattle prod. I recognize the smell, the sound, the punch.

Before I'm even down, there's another one up at the back of my neck.

Another flashbulb pop, followed by the sizzle.

I waver, my hands still aiming my dick, and fall forward into the mess.

This isn't how it's supposed to happen, I want to tell them, Singer's goons.

This isn't how it goes.

But. One of them is standing on my left hand, grinding. The other's got his instep of his prettyboy loafer around the arch of my neck, pushing my face down into the stink.

Because I can't hear anything yet, they wait.

Finally my body heaves and a line of puke peters out. I swallow some of it back down and it makes me puke again, so that it's coming out my nose, even.

"You're dead," I finally tell them, when I can.

It's a joke. They laugh.

On the kitchen floor, unfolded, staring along the floor at me, is the Dead Vegetable Ghost.

They came to see why he wasn't finishing his rounds. Maybe there really is a restaurant grease racket.

"You're making things difficult for yourself," the one with his foot on my neck rumbles. It's a prepared script, I can tell. "There's no need to bite the hand that feeds you," the other chimes in.

"Dead," I say again, the word making bubbles in the carpet.

"Just don't let it happen again," the first one says, pushing harder as he steps away.

I don't move, won't give them that.

"Or we'll be back," the second one says.

"Promise?" I manage.

The muscles in my back are still twitchy, misfiring.

"Guaranteed," he says, and comes gently off my hand.

It's the mistake people always make. When you've got somebody down, you cripple them at the very least. Make it so they can't stand.

My throbbing hand comes up like a snake, to drive through what, if he were a woman, would be his birthing canal. To reach into his belly, pull his guts out all at once, wrap them around the other sap's neck, bring him to his knees and make him beg.

Except that first one already has his cattle prod to my lower back.

It fires, curls me up, leaves me smoking.

They stand over me talking about I don't know what. One of them strikes a cigarette up just for a single pull then grinds it out slow on the back of my head.

I'm there enough to know it's happening, not there enough to feel it yet.

And then they're just black-slacked legs standing in the kitchen, with orders to get my next list, give it to the New Vegetable Ghost.

"Dead," I try to say again, but don't know if it makes it past my lips.

And then I'm gone.

That afternoon, still stumbly, I accidentally call Riley by the Girl Scout name. She moans about it, maybe even moves her leg. I close my eyes, apologize. Let her run her hand over my head, just shaved. Not to hide who I am, or who I was to let them get the drop on me like that, but to get away from the smell of burnt hair.

I am going to kill those two.

Anybody with black slacks, really.

At least the marble finally passes, a little tink against the porcelain, like I've been eating teeth again. I don't save it, just let it swirl away.

The muscles in my shoulders are still jumpy.

I've checked the rattletrap connected to the lefthand front door probably thirty times already, and managed to run a ground wire from it to my kitchen light, as backup, the kitchen light's usual ground just hanging.

Now if somebody opens the door in the lefthand apartment, my light'll go dark.

Every time it zapped me, too, I just bared my teeth back at it.

It was nothing. Neither were those punks. Just lucky is all.

Except I know it's her fault, Dashboard Mary's.

Finally, halfway through boiling some squash Singer probably had to fly in from Mexico, I take the phone, highlight the last call and hit the green button.

It rings five perfect times, dumps me to her message box.

Another trap, I know: since Kid Hoodie's recording of my voice is still here with me, she's trying to get another.

But she needs to know this, too.

"You're no nurse," I hiss, just a pushed-through whisper that could be anybody anywhere, judge. Not even my phone.

I'm onto her stupid game.

Those weren't orderlies next door. Those weren't syringes they were poking into my back. And if it was institutionalized electroshock, I would have at least had something to bite down on, I'm pretty sure.

After the call's over and done with I stare at the little screen, daring her to call back. Daring her to call ever again at all.

Instead, just the same blinking from yesterday.

The last voice mail she left.

I shake my head, stir my squash. Stand in the steam and listen.

It makes the message I just left stupid.

She's not pretending to be a nurse anymore. End of that charade.

What she's doing now is warning me.

Evidently two men were just standing on the sidewalk of my building. They were talking on a cell phone, taking orders. Keeping close enough to the brick that, from my window, they wouldn't even be there at all.

And now one of them was looking up, to the idea of me, and the other was clapping the cell phone shut, nodding, and now they're extracting this long suitcase from their trunk, not opening it outdoors for her to see what it is they're bringing upstairs with them.

I'm supposed to be careful. To watch out.

From his crooked place under the table, by the wall, I can hear Kid Hoodie breathing through the nostril he has that isn't folded over, pinched shut.

It's raspy and strained.

I walk along the edge of the rug to the window, look out from high up on the left side.

I can see in as far as the curb below me, no deeper.

A fire hydrant, a stoop with a metal railing. What used to be a place where a tree was but's just a grate now.

Across from me, the old man with his telescope pretends to be looking into one of the windows on the second or third floor.

I pull my curtain shut, sit down in the corner, listen to Kid Hoodie's rasp. Watch the front door. Only pull my squash off the burner when I think the smoke alarm's going to go off again.

It's not even self-preservation when I do it, either.

I think it's just that I don't want that skater punk to get in trouble again. Sometimes I'm a stranger even to myself.

That's good, though. Keep them guessing.

I shrug it off, that thanks the skater punk's not ever going to give me, just cook another batch of out-of-season squash, chew it more times than it needs chewing, swallow the paste down. The next mouthful is slower, though. Of course. Nobody can see, but I nod, smile. Take another heaping bite.

Dashboard Mary.

She wasn't calling because she cared about me, or to get on my good side, or to make up for past wrongs. She was calling because she doesn't want Singer cutting in front of her. She's worked too long to lose me now.

I lift a forkful of yellow up to the window, commend her.

We're more alike than she thinks.

Without meaning to—who would, right?—I dip my head a couple of times while sitting in my chair in the sun, then snap it back up.

The second time, I see what's happening.

To make it better, I guide the wet-dry vac back to its place, throw a jacket over the table Kid Hoodie's under, a blanket over the base of the coat rack. Angle the curtains just so.

There. Yeah.

It's a month ago, now.

Nothing different from right before Kid Hoodie knocked on my door.

This is where it all starts.

I nod, lower myself back to the chair slowly. This is how you settle into the past. At least the body part of you. The room around that body. It takes hours to get my head there.

But finally.

I wasn't in the game, I know that, and I wasn't next door petting Riley, and I had my pants on and zipped. The wet-dry vac was in the back room, its cord stapled to the wall. Maybe it was straining against it, sure—you have to assume it always is—but I wasn't even looking down the mouth of the hall for it.

What I was doing was staring. Straight ahead. Into that slant of light coming in through the window.

It was peaceful. Had been two hours maybe since I'd last moved. Time had gotten all sludgy around me. I was still in the moment, but the moment I was in, it was hours long.

And then—yeah.

That's it.

I'd just eaten three artichokes slimy with butter.

It was too much for one sitting, but it was on purpose too.

That's why I was so still.

I'd eaten the artichokes sitting right in the chair, which is bad form if you live alone, no ritual, nothing to separate this action out from the rest, and then I'd just set the plate on the side table. Later it would be crusty, but that would be later. And worth it.

And the artichokes. Juicy flowers from another planet. What cactus looks like on Mars. The perfect choice for what I was doing.

Before I'd stopped moving, I'd placed the fingertips of one hand over my stomach, my other fingertips lower down, spread across my gut like spider legs.

The plan was to get in touch with my digestion once and for all.

It was a yoga thing, but it really came from watching worms as a kid, I think. I used to be pretty sure that they were just these long writhy stomachs, that all they did, the only sensations they could know, was the dirt they ate, passing through them.

I had been so jealous.

To have just one sensation, a single purpose?

Then you'd never have to choose what to do. Never have to decide if what you were feeling was good or bad or what. It just would be the way it was, end of story.

Some of my early experimenting with girls was along these lines.

But I wasn't thinking of that then, a month ago.

I was being a worm, being *the* worm. Every fiber, every pore.

On purpose, even, I'd barely even chewed the artichoke. The idea was that the nerve endings on my insides, they probably didn't know to be sensitive. So if the artichoke still had sharp edges, I'd be able to feel it better along its switchback route.

Not chewing, though, yeah.

My jaws don't butterfly open like a snakes, sorry.

That's why all the butter.

Still though, my eyes had watered each time I swallowed.

But it was all going to be worth it.

I was going to be different this time. I was going—sitting there in my chair, the sun warming me, my scrubbed fingertips making me twice as aware of what I was doing, it was going to make me different. Better. Not a man who thinks like a worm, but a worm moving among men. With a single purpose.

It's where I'd been going my whole life.

But then, only two hours into it, the artichokes just gathering at the bottom mouth of my stomach, the butter already churning below, greasing the chute, my arm and hand numb, every bit of my awareness gathered in my fingertips, the door had knocked.

I don't even think I heard it that first time.

Going through it a second time now, though, I have no choice—and I've got time, aren't even scheduled to say anything about pizza until the next knock—no choice but to backtrace Kid Hoodie. Before he was Kid Hoodie.

Jason Pease.

It all starts on a ferry for him.

He's standing there at the railing, thinking how the film on top of the water, how what if it ever dried into a crust, would there be different kinds of fish then, would the mice with the most webbed feet learn to run across it, the cats splashing through behind them, but he doesn't get to finish.

Someone's watching him, her hair swishing behind her.

A woman with a billowy shirt. Clacky boots. Dinner plate sunglasses.

She doesn't tell him about me at first either.

At first she just traces her collarbone for some reason, already has a newspaper cocked under her arm. It's an invitation. Jason Pease takes it, asks if she's read his article today.

Of course she has—but, that's yours? Really?

After that it's just the usual: drinks, lunch, dinner, all spread across the week. He shows her his desk at work, she shows him her bed.

The whole time, though, she's carrying something inside her.

Not the rumor of me, up here above the city, a myth, a legend, a story-in-the-making for the right journalist, but an empty, calloused place somewhere on her, probably covered by clothes or make-up or the way she laughs.

It's the scar from whoever I took away from her. Her reason for giving herself to this Jason Pease with his stupid music and his cigarette breath and his slouchy way of walking into a room. What she has now is this little crater of skin where she used to be connected to somebody.

I want to place my mouth there.

It's on her side, I'd guess. Right above her hips, and to the back a little.

With my mouth there, I could look up into her eyes. She could stroke my hair down, the marble in the bottle on her wrist winking.

But then Jason Pease is knocking for the second time. About to become Kid Hoodie.

The base of my scalp by my neck trembles, and I hear myself answering already: *You order pizza?*

My voice, too, it's the recording. Tinny and distant, coming from the feet of the coat rack.

I rise, touch the same five things on the way to the door, being careful they're not the easy things, and Kid Hoodie's there with his clay face, his plastic caster feet.

"She sent me," he says.

I nod, tell him I know, and step aside.

He rolls in, his head already ducked between his shoulder blades because he knows what's coming.

"You'll need this," he tells me, palming his phone over, "and these," unhooking the ear buds, dragging them from his hood.

He's crying a little too, I think. Dirty grey tears rolling down his face, making my carpet dingy like ash.

"Tell me about the boat again," he says, and I do: growing up, I remember how this one kid's mom cried and cried because she thought her son was on a ferry that went down, but then I told her he hadn't been, and she hugged me so hard my feet came off the ground. I cried a little too.

But it's a lie.

Her son was on that ferry.

Only, instead of sinking—here I'm looking out the window instead of into Kid Hoodie's hood, and he's looking out the window with me, following—this beautiful woman approached him on the deck where neither of them were supposed to be standing, and bared her side for him, a sore there that wasn't even oozing anymore, had dried up. But still, he fell into it, drowned, and she just pulled her shirt back down, clacked back to stand by the exit door.

Kid Hoodie nods when I'm done like he agrees, that that's

probably the way it went, and then tries to rake my pinky with his, so that maybe they'll catch together, be locked.

I don't let that happen, though.

I step back, bury the dirty little axe high up in his neck.

His head folds forward onto his chest, and I see that his spine, wiggling there, *it's* the worm, but by the time I reach for it it's already back down into his body.

This isn't how it's supposed to go, either.

Not at all.

What I feel like, sitting in the chair, the sun hours gone, my robot sleeves back on but not working right, is that the game is real, but I don't understand it.

The television networks did band together, hire their pedophile.

But it wasn't so I could help them with their programming.

Down in my presidential bomb shelter under the city, in my glass apartment suspended by cable, I'm the star of their show.

Every day people are glued to their screens, watching me go through my daily business, watching me think I'm—

I'm . . .

I don't know.

They watch me think I'm not in a hospital, and they laugh.

They watch the ghosts in the other rooms of the Chessire Arms, and they laugh with them.

They watch the actor pretending to be Singer, straightening his crime boss suit in the other room, and they gasp and clap at the introduction, by popular demand, of a love interest.

I shake my head no, please.

Dashboard Mary.

I close my eyes, shake my head, bury my face in my hands and, like when Kid Hoodie came that first time, I don't hear the phone when it rings under the blanket.

By the time I get there, it's another voice mail.

Her.

"Knock-knock," she whispers.

The audience gasps with pleasure.

To make sure I'm all the way back to where I'm supposed to be, I eat three more artichokes. But first I make myself wait for them to cook.

They taste like candle wax and salt. I swallow them as whole as I can, so that they cut my throat coming back up, make me think of giant dry asparagus heads pointed the wrong direction.

I grind them in all three disposals then flush them once, wait for the tank to fill, and do it four more times again.

I'm here.

Shaky, but if somebody knocks, I'll know it this time. If anybody's standing behind me, I'll know that too.

Because I'm careful—her boyfriend already risked it all, and lost, just to get my voice on tape—I dump my last half loaf of sourdough bread from the soft plastic bag, unwrap it from its crinkly shell. The crinkly bag goes around the phone, for static. When that's not good enough, I pack the microphone part with a fingernail of leftover clay I have to get wet, but that won't work. She won't be able to hear me at all. With an old phone, I could plug every other hole if I wanted.

But you make do with what you have.

I dig the clay out with a toothpick, extract Kid Hoodie from his crooked place under the table.

147

"Your neck must be killing you," I say to him, and can't help smiling.

He won't even look at me.

"Nothing personal," I tell him, and lean forward, bite as much of his grey right eyebrow off as I can.

At first I gag from the crumbly taste, have to bury my chin deep in my chest to keep the heaves down. But I've had worse things in my mouth. And I don't even have to swallow this, just have to pack it all around, like the ceramic in a catalytic converter.

I say it out loud, her name, Dashboard Mary, and just with the clay and my artichoked throat, I already sound different enough. Add the crackle of the sourdough wrap, and I'm nobody, I'm everybody. Not tomorrow's headline.

I don't even need to put the wet-dry vac sleeves on to push the callback button, either.

"I'm calling her," I say to the old man with the telescope. To show him, I lower the phone from my mouth, point at it with my other hand. He doesn't nod or look away or pretend to be doing something else, and for an instant the bottom drops out of my stomach: what if—what if he's like my downstairs family? A mannequin in a wheelchair, the telescope propped there beside him.

A scarecrow.

For me.

The whole building posed just for me, for me to think I'm in the real part of town.

Of course there aren't any cars on the street. It's not because of parking, but because mannequins don't have anywhere to go.

But there'd have to be somebody real over there.

Another—no, not another Vegetable Ghost. Probably *my* Vegetable Ghost, before I snuffed him. His whole job was me.

Drop off supplies, check. Pick up corpse drum, check. Take anxiety meds, check. Go next door, move mannequin arms and change curtains for five hours, check.

I should have been watching out my window for the past two days already. Seeing if anything's changing, or if the building's just become a painting, one I could probably walk behind, see the blank canvas of if I wanted.

Shit.

No.

I shake my head about it, that this is—that it wouldn't be a good money decision, for Singer to rent out a whole building. Or, to own it, and *not* rent it out. To have all the lights on timers, the timers plugged into sockets that are hot, the meter just rolling and rolling.

But it all comes back to that dog you drag into the alley because it bit your kid on the face.

What *wouldn't* you do?

The kneejerk thing's just to have some fun with the dog for a few hours. But after those few hours are gone, and you're shoulder deep in shit and blood and whatever else you brought to the table, still, your kid's face isn't any less fucked up, right?

At which point you start backing up to that alley again. That dog. Wishing you'd made it last longer, maybe. Not let your anger get the better of you.

I smile to myself, tears hot in the corner of my eyes.

What you'd wish is that you'd been nice to that dog, maybe. Led it back to your place, then, I don't know. Held bites of stew meat out to it every other day or so, then jolted the shit out of it every third time it reached out for that bite, at least until it learns. Then change it to every fourth time.

Or shave it bare, grease it up, stake it out in the sun. See if a dog can get skin cancer.

Or—or lock it up. Never give it any contact with its own kind again. Just traipse cardboard cut-outs of other dogs past it sometimes, so that it starts sniffing them, rubbing their throats with the top of its head. Finally testing them with its teeth, then ripping them apart. Every single one that you trot up.

And then, at the end of it, you open the door of its kennel, so that it can go free.

Only, all over the lawn, you've staked down these real dogs. But the dog that bit your kid, it can't tell the difference anymore. Thinks the whole world's cardboard. Is afraid to leave.

You'd have to really have loved your kid to go to all that trouble, I mean.

Or your yoga instructor.

I shut my eyes tight, pray for the old man across the way to move, and into that darkness Mary says it again, right into my head: "Knock-knock?"

I don't know how long she's been on.

I gravel my voice up, try to keep the sob out of it, and say my part back to her: "Who's there?"

"Police," she says.

"Police who?" I say back weaker but cringing, unable not to finish the damn joke I've been waiting on for so long.

"Pu-lease give my husband back," she says.

We don't laugh.

The tear at the edge of my eye rolls down, and I wipe it away.

I shake my head no, no. That I'm not twelve years old here. And that I'm not Singer's dog.

I crinkle the plastic, try to stand but the little phone's still plugged in.

Kid Hoodie snickers, looks away.

I scoot forward, kick my chair at him.

On the line there's just silence. Listening. Waiting.

"He the pizza boy or the flower kid?" I finally manage. "Your husband."

Again, silence.

She's crying too, I think.

Probably has a picture of him right there.

"You're right," she says, her voice hardly cracking. "I'm not a nurse."

"Nurses wear white," I tell her. "Not—"

"Black, yeah," she cuts in, getting better now too. "Ha ha. What should I call you?"

I narrow my eyes, study the table.

"Since we're such good friends," I say.

"I'm Mary," she says.

"I know."

She doesn't say anything.

"Jack, then," I finally pick from the air like a gnat. In some language it probably means chump.

Again from her end: not much.

"Something wrong?" I ask after a couple of breaths, holding the phone away from my face to look at it.

"No," she says, but it's thready and weak. "*Jack*," she repeats then, like a holy word, like she's tasting it. "The one always pretending to be something he's not, you mean?"

"Come and knock on my door," I tell her. "I've been waiting for you."

She breathes a harsh little laugh out, it sounds like. Her pressure release valve. Then changes the phone to the other side of her head. Maybe taking her earring out like girls will. Or pulling her hair into a bun. Standing to walk from room to room.

I stay in my place by the coat rack, my singed hair spread all over the floor in the bathroom.

"What was *his* name?" I ask.

"My husband."

"Your husband."

"You keep a list or something, I guess?"

"Makes it easier for the cops."

She switches ears again. Maybe does a neat little flipturn at the counter to her kitchen, paces back down the hall to her bedroom.

It's because when she stands still, she can feel me looking at her. Into her.

"You're doing something to your voice," she finally says.

"I'm not stupid, if that's what you're getting at."

"I never thought you were."

"Said the pretty nurse."

She gives me that.

"You could have done this without him," I tell her. "Kid Hoodie. But thanks, I guess."

She stops walking, looks into the phone.

". . . Kid who?"

I rub my eyes, hate myself more than just a little. "Pease, Jason. The paper boy."

"Him. He doesn't matter."

"Never did."

"Then you do save their names," she says.

I shrug, look around my baseboard. Study the floor in front of the front door but light never comes in there anymore. It'd be unfair, to be able to see shadow legs. Unfair, and I'd never be able to look away from it, would watch it instead of my shows, instead of eating, instead of anything.

If you don't know yourself, you don't know shit.

"He was a good man, my husband," she says, quieter but more sure of herself. "A good cop."

I nod, should have guessed.

Only a cop's wife could have taken it this far.

They're really big into the parade funerals, I mean. Flag, guns, somebody getting the needle on the jumbo screen, all that shit.

Her husband, though, I probably could have fit him into a cup when I was done with him.

"A good *father*," she adds, like that's supposed to be the thing that breaks me.

I shrug again, my eyes flat, dry now.

She's just another person at the door. Somebody else to play Trouble with. Or Sorry.

No, not Sorry. Risk.

"You're name's not Jack, either," she says.

"Why not?"

"We almost named our daughter after him, you know? Jacqueline. Jackie."

"I don't follow."

"You have to be part of the human race, I guess."

It's another joke. We both laugh a bit.

"One thing humans do, see, is name their kids after themselves. Like a gift."

I nod, get it, why she'd programmed that song in, why she can't let my name be Jack: "*His* name was Jack."

"Almost matched his badge number," she says, her mouth not so close to the phone anymore.

"And you want me to what, here? Apologize? Honor his name after . . . well. After whatever?"

"I didn't have to tell you about those men coming up to your place."

"I don't owe you anything, babe."

"*Babe*," she spits back, with something like another laugh.

"So his name was Jack," I lead off. "I'm going to need more. I'm in kind of a high-volume business here, if you know what I mean."

Really, there's only ever been one uniform, so I already know. But I burned his credentials over and over, finally ate them myself, because I was sure Singer was finally setting me up.

It was early on, when I was always worried. Doing stupid shit left and right.

But his name, it's gone, dust.

And I guess there could have been another cop or two, in plainclothes, but they didn't have identification on them anyway. And, if they were undercover, trying to slouch their way into Singer's trust, it would have been some dummied, dumbed-down identification. Screw it.

"Maybe I could dig his personal effects up or something," I add. "Give him back that way, at least. Been meaning to thin the collection down some anyway. My mom always said I was a packrat."

Does she consider it?

No.

"You already told me you're not stupid," she says.

"I'm not even human, according to you."

"Widows have a limited perspective, I guess you could say."

"So?"

"So what?"

"So now you've got me on the phone. Aren't you supposed to be messing with my mind or something? Big psychological campaign? Get me caught, make me kill myself, all that?"

"You're doing that just fine without me," she says.

I tighten my lips, stare into the carpet.

She coughs a laugh through the line.

Which one am I doing *fine* at, the getting caught or the killing myself?

But she probably wants me to ask.

154

Fuck her. Every last one of her.

"He asked for you at the end," I say through the plastic, through the clay, over my bloody throat and into the little phone. "For you and her both."

This finally makes her breathe hard.

"One call," she threatens. "One call—"

"That you could have made last year," I finish for her. "Instead of getting your boyfriend all, you know. Troubled."

"He wasn't my—"

"He didn't matter, right. Just another delivery boy."

Silence, ungolden silence.

"I can't talk now," she says from her place in the hall, I'm pretty sure. Slid down the wall so she's sitting, her knees up by her face. A long curl wrapped around and around her index finger. Or the phone cord, if she's on an old phone.

"So what'd you end up naming her?" I say.

She's crying now. Way back in her throat where she doesn't want to. I can hear it so clear, so wonderful.

"Wouldn't you like to know," she says back, and hangs up hard.

Score one for the home team.

I push the red button, walk from room to room nodding to myself.

One call, she said, but she won't.

This is between her and me.

I run every word of our talk through my head over and over, until I have to eat something. But the vegetables are all two days old now. Gone, as far as I'm concerned.

Because I don't want the bread to go fuzzy on the counter, I just eat it instead, piece by piece with mustard and pepper until I can't hold anymore.

There's still two slices left at the end, the heel and the one sloping down to the heel.

I put them on a saucer, carry them next door to Riley like a birthday cake, and the only reason I even start fiddling with the badge around my neck is because she takes so long to chew. And then I stop fiddling.

Riley tucks herself away from my stillness, the bread just a soggy lump in her mouth now.

I pet her hair down, hum like she likes.

The badge.

The first four numbers of it are 5-2-2-4.

On the little phone—I know because I've been studying it— those numbers can spell *Jacg*. Or *Jach*. *Jaci*.

Almost Jack.

She thinks I killed him.

And now I know her daughter's name too.

The next morning I do everything in the lefthand apartment but open the door, look down the hall. The vegetables here are old too. I can't trust them anymore.

This doesn't happen.

I could starve this way.

Finally I decide that the reason there's not any dolly wheels rolling up the hall from the elevator is that I haven't prepared the apartment enough.

So I clean. And clean. The pee, the blood, the shit and gore and tears. Light the vanilla candles that have always been in the cabinet above the dishwasher.

The smoke is thick like burning sugar, and so it won't get in the hall, gum up the fire alarms, get an inspector up here to talk safety with the residents of the Chessire Arms, I roll up a wet towel longwise, stuff it against the crack under the door.

That works for about ten minutes. Until I gag the first time.

I pry the outside window up, let the apartment breathe.

As for the candles, I remember that flames like oxygen, so I line them up on the sill. The idea is they'll pull all the sweet air to them, and it'll get sucked outside.

Nobody's ever thought of this, I'm pretty sure.

I could have been anything, I mean.

I guess I already am, though.

And I don't let the candles burn all the way down to their foil bases either, of course.

Halfway through the job, the air clear enough that I can see the blood I missed in the pattern of the linoleum, it hits me again, that those candles have *always* been there.

One by one I take them to the kitchen, smush them under the creaky rolling pin, to see what tracking devices or microphones they might have.

Zero, it turns out, but you can never be too safe.

The next thirty minutes involve wrapping my hands in dishtowels and rolling all the wax crumbles thinner and thinner, into a paste, then a film. Because the top layer of it was stupid with my fingerprints.

Now, as thin as it is, it's a trap. Anybody comes over, leans right there to read the small word I've written on the board (*gotcha*), I'll know. And they'll never find the rolling pin to make it like it was.

Next, like clockwork, what I want to do is try the door to the hall. Because maybe the door won't even open with the wet towel right there. And the Newest Vegetable Ghost, he's probably been told specifically not to knock, right?

Would I be able to hear the knob turning?

The only way to tell would be to turn the knob.

Instead I take the towel up, hang it off one of the pegs in the wall so it won't stink the place up. Then I hang it off both pegs, so that it looks more like wings, but then I adjust it so it's just a towel again. Because if it's wings, that would put the face of that angel through the wall, looking at me next door with its never blinking eyes. Its gold-flecked pupils.

No thanks.

I do get as far as touching the knob once, my other four

fingers resting on the molding beside it, in proper sequence front to back and over again, stopping at the knob like's right, but it would be the worst luck to turn it, at least from the inside. Bad precedence.

And the little phone, of course, it's in my pocket. Just to be sure I'll hear it ring, feel it, I don't have underwear on today. Don't need that extra layer between me and it. To squelch any extra rustle, I shaved all my pubic hair down too. It'll grow back faster than my head hair. The moist dark is good for that.

Still, none of that's made the little phone ring yet. And I've been charging it every forty-five minutes. Just to be sure. Checking the call log, the ring settings, the volume.

Nothing.

But I can't push that green button either.

It's her turn to call.

Let her think we're talking on her terms, that's the ticket.

That way when I pull the rug out from under her life she'll have that much further to fall.

Your husband, the reason you've been on my case for the past two years? I didn't even do him.

And, that girl you almost named after him, who did you end up naming her after? What's it say on her headstone now? Anybody in your family ever go by Ryland, something like that? What's that, you kind of slipped away there.

A lesser person would be jacking off already, just thinking about this.

Not me. You've got to save it for when it counts.

And the lack of rubber wheels in the hall, that's nothing. It just means that Singer's still interviewing potential ghosts, trying to find that perfect balance between expendable and reliable.

I can make it for a day or two without anything fresh. Food or otherwise.

And if it's punishment for letting the last Vegetable Ghost die, then fuck it.

Never would have happened if there'd been somebody standing at my threshold instead.

Not my fault.

And I may not even need him right now anyway.

Riley.

It's the secret word, the one that'll bring somebody to my door.

Knock-knock, I'll say from my side.

I know it's you, she'll say back.

Knock-knock, I'll insist, giving back what she gave me.

From the hall, crying. The sides of fists hitting the opposite wall. A pistol as long as her arm in her purse, probably.

It's going to take more than that, babe.

Who's there? she'll finally cough out.

Jack, I'll tell her, my mouth right to the crack of the door, the badge around my neck clinking against the paint.

Let me see her, she'll say.

On the couch, propped up, Riley. In the Girl Scout uniform.

Jack's not here, I'll say back, and then lower myself to the loose lip of the carpet on my side of the door. The carpet Dashboard Mary's standing on, cut loose on each side of her, just half an inch thinner than the door, then ducking under to my side. Just enough force, a double hand, a hard push.

From down the hall, if there's a kid watching around the corner, stocking his nightmares, this is what it'll look like: a woman flailing her arms suddenly up, juggling a huge pistol to her chest just in time for her back to slam into the ground.

Her boots, though, they're already in the maw of the door.

And something has them, is pulling her through, to her destiny.

Sleep well, kid.

The first part of dressing Riley is getting the Girl Scout uniform out of the oven. I pretend it's a safe I'm cracking, roll the controls left a few clicks, right a certain amount more, then all the way around twice.

Bingo.

I give Kid Hoodie a fake thumbs up.

When he won't even shrug back, I go directly to him, fling the table out of the way and then drag him up, carry him by the scalp over to the counter. Slam him neckdown onto it, so he sticks.

I work the little phone up from my pocket, push the green button twice to dial Dashboard Mary and smush the phone into his clay ear.

After today, he's gone.

One thing I don't need around the place is some smartass, always judging me from whatever corner he's in.

"Tell her all about it," I say to him, mushing the phone around.

From somewhere in there, her voice, "Is that you?"

"Jason," I say, loud enough that maybe she hears.

But maybe not.

I leave the phone there, Kid Hoodie staring the other way, and go back to the oven, rip the door open.

The Girl Scout uniform is right where I left it, folded back on itself just like it was in the brown box.

If I put it to my nose, would I smell the Girl Scout, or Dashboard Mary?

I try, just get artichoke aftertaste. From when I was cooking on the stovetop. The fumes must get trapped in here somehow.

It doesn't matter.

Soon enough I'll be able to take her by the shirt, pull her close, my face in her neck, and draw in all the scent I want. And it'll be better then. More afraid. She'll be breathing hard.

My hand goes down to my pants again, my crotch, but no.

Not yet.

Instead I go back to the storage unit with Belinda. Those two days alone, to dispose of the evidence. Like the way some dads'll make you smoke the whole pack of cigarettes if they even catch you with one.

For most kids, I guess that works.

But those two days, the between times, my guts roiling, so dark I couldn't even see my fingers before my face, I went back to the breathing Belinda had been doing. So even, like a metronome. A pendulum. In, out, in out, deep now, exhale, swallow, swallow, all of it collecting in my head like the surf, pushing a line of foam closer and closer to me, to whisper up between my fingers and then slip away, the sand under me clean again.

Yeah.

Some of the people you escort out of the world, it's just a job, something to occupy your afternoon. Others, though, others you learn a little something from. So it's like they never die, really. At least not until you do. And in spite of what they wished with their last breaths, or said with their eyes right before their pupils went all fixed and dilated, focused on something I always thought was right behind me but never could turn fast enough to see.

Thank you, I'm saying. Thank you, Belinda.

Without you, none of this.

Now, exhale, stretch.

The Girl Scout uniform's just that: some clothes. Nothing much at all. And Riley'll like it anyway. It'll make her feel pretty.

I should say thank you to Dashboard Mary, when I see her.

A guy forgets this kind of stuff—clothes, pretty shit.

And girls, young ones, they need a woman around.

It's funny, that. 'Around.'

Something like that, yeah.

I laugh a bit, everything's going so right, and stand with the uniform. Take it by the shoulders and shake it unfolded, to see if it's going to be big enough.

But then.

Fluttering to the ground from each fold is a photograph. A snapshot. All different ones, looted from some old album.

The kind that get set up at funerals sometimes, so everybody can remember this is a celebration, that they don't have to be sad.

Good pictures, I mean. Of the good times. Which is what you're supposed to remember.

It's her husband, the one I never even met. *Jack* in cursive on the back of some—the name I lucked onto, that she thought she'd already given me. But I never even looked until now, swear.

She'll give me him at this barbecue, at that police function, in front of whatever Christmas tree, but she couldn't bring herself to let me see his face. She's keeping that for herself, in some salt shaker or pill bottle.

All the faces are cut out. Neat little ovals of nothing.

It's supposed to tell me what I've done, I think.

There's even some of him holding baby Riley.

I don't touch any of them, can't, but I do lower myself to study those ones anyway.

If I had any pictures of myself, I could cut my face out, paste it there. Frame it for Riley to look at when I'm not there.

Camera, I want to write on the board in the lefthand apartment.

Except you don't do that. You don't leave pictures of yourself at the crime scene, at what will be a crime scene if you ever hear a SWAT team pounding up the hallway.

Maybe I'll just cut baby Riley out, then. Mat it against a black sheet of paper. Tell her I've been keeping it in my wallet for years. That, next door, I have the television on so they'll think I'm just living, but really, I've been staring at this one snapshot. For years.

Because I love you.

This is another thing to thank Mary for.

On the way into the closet, the little door that opens onto the righthand apartment, I touch five things, so that I can bring that strength with me to dress Riley.

It'll be my first time, putting clothes on one of them.

Every day, it's a new thing.

I hum my way over to her bed, tell her that Daddy's here, and then prop her up as gently as I can, start the process.

Instead of eating a dinner of imaginary vegetables, I clean the little phone up. Make sure it still holds a charge. Check the voice mail.

There is one, of course.

She's just there. Not saying anything.

I don't know.

Before, with the cookies, with the ringtones, the nurse shit. It was all part of some mindfuck. Was supposed to get me asking so many questions in my head that I finally had to just take a knife, cut them out to get a proper grip on them.

That's over now.

And the pictures on my kitchen floor, I was supposed to have already seen them. And, two days ago, who knows. They might have got to me in some way. Now, they're nothing. Like throwing lit matches into a house fire.

Is that what she wants me to think, though?

Maybe the mindfuck's over, but there's something new. Maybe what I'm supposed to do is hold each one of these, study it. Maybe her whole plan depends on pretending to get lured here, then asking for one of the pictures, make some point about it, then storm out before I can do anything. Because, I don't know. Because she's holding something over me. Is going to tell Singer about the Girl Scout who skated, the Green Paper Suit guy. If he wasn't hers in the first place.

And then she'd have my fingerprints on that picture. Then she'd have everything.

But I'm not stupid either. This is exactly where she wants me, cornered in my own head. Not sure if everything's one way or another.

Trick is, I don't really need to know, I don't guess.

Sit on somebody's chest, your knees in the hollow under their collarbone, your thumbs hard against their windpipe, and the whole rest of the world can be dinosaurs who bake birthday cakes. It won't change what's going on under my hands. What's happening to her.

But I've made promises to myself, too. Right-before-sleep kind of promises. So I *can* sleep.

I'm not going to do it fast. Not all at once anyway.

And as much as I can, I'm going to let her watch most of it.

One thing I've always thought would work is to shoot one of them up with something that doesn't let them feel anything. So they're just a head. And lay them out on a table and hang a sheet from the ceiling right at their neckline. Then, maybe with a camera, maybe with mirrors—this'll all take time, a long list on the board—let whoever it is (her) watch on a screen, or in the reflection.

Trick is, and they won't know this of course, is that what I'm really doing with the knives and probes and toys, I'm doing it to somebody else. Or to a dog, even. Anything with blood, so that when I pull the kidney out of its sac, they think it's their kidney.

Will they still be able to pee then, or will their brain click over into some other mode?

I've got interests, see.

And then I'll do this a time or two, and show them their own uncut belly afterwards, but then on some special day, when I'm in the mood, am tired of all the things I fool them into thinking I'm doing, I'll dust their stomach with powder, so that they think it's the cadaver, but then really cut on *them*.

After that, it's as simple as pretending to pass out where they can see, or shoot myself—they'll believe anything if it gets you on the floor—so that they can swing off the table, run for the door.

Only—only they're tripping on something, what?

Yeah.

And then I stand up behind them, wait for them to crane their neck around. Wait for them to know the truth, their last truth. The shape of it, leaning down to take them by the hair, drag them into the real world.

It's what's going to make this dry month worth it.

"You get that?" I say into the phone. Into the recording of Dashboard Mary, still just breathing, just there.

Didn't think so.

Later that night, when I'm probably supposed to be asleep, I hear footsteps on my ceiling. It's the first time ever.

I stand in the living room, the wet-dry vac sleeves on again, and reach straight up, place my fingertips to the crackly paint.

The apartment up there's supposed to be empty. Supposed to be for later. Because if you explore your whole world all at once, what do you do with the rest of the years, right? There always needs to be something left to discover. Otherwise you turn your knife inwards, think there must be another cave just under your sternum, maybe. Or, if not there, in the hollow under your left arm.

Thanks but no thanks.

And anyway, I don't have any hollow places left, I don't think. They were all wallowed out by the time I was fifteen.

Ever since then, I've just been trying to fill them back in, pretty much. Tamp down over them.

But maybe this is the night. For discovery.

It's her up there, I know.

Maybe the plan is to just move in, homestead the place. Make me listen to her clacky heels until I have to complain to management like I'm just another lackwit. One who can't take care of things himself.

Not likely.

I drag a chair into the bedroom, prop it into the closet, then stand there, my gas mask already on. The chainsaw starts on the second pull, like always.

I cut a ragged circle, pull myself up through it before the dust has even settled, and understand now why I've been wearing the wet-dry vac sleeves. They keep the splinters and nails from the fishbelly parts of my arms.

Nobody's waiting for me when I step out of the closet.

Through the mask's goggles, this could be my bedroom too. Maybe will be, years down the road. If I ever decide to be closer to the roof.

No time for reminiscing about the future, though.

I leave the chainsaw on, lead with it into the hall and, when it's empty, the living room.

Hanging by the neck, framed in the window, some woman.

I back away, knock the kitchen table half over, then am suddenly sure whoever did that to her's in the kitchen, on the other side of the counter.

I saw a wide V into it, kick the front part away so it falls half against the opposite counter, cocking the refrigerator door open enough to spill light down onto the linoleum, as far back as the shallow pantry.

There's nobody.

And the hanging woman, she's still just hanging. Though I'm ready, one hundred percent ready for her to turn around, climb down off that rope. Spider across the ceiling, try to pull me up there with her.

I back out of the kitchen, try the front door. Locked. I nod to myself like I expected this too, then crab walk back the way I came, my ass to the wall the whole way.

Has anybody on the fifth floor heard all this? Already called me in?

If I could go to the window, I could check for red and blue lights coming in from every spoke of the city. And this is just how they'd want me, too: in a mask, armored sleeves, chainsaw grinding the air.

After two more minutes of the hanging woman just hanging, I let the chainsaw spin down, go quiet.

In the hall, as near as I can hear—it's not my hall, though, so I'm not sure what's normal—there's no fast footsteps. No worried brows. No questions.

But just because you can't hear it, yeah.

I'm not stupid.

And the—

No.

The bottle hanging from the woman's wrist. In it there aren't any flashing red and blue lights. Just the marble, trying to find a place to settle.

I shake my head no, fall to my knees a little but push back up with the chainsaw, suddenly an old man with a cane.

But it could still be a trick.

But there's only way to know, too.

Walking as slow as any kid ever has to his punishment, I cross the living room, take the woman by the hand.

It doesn't close back over my fingers, is cool, plastic.

The mannequin rotates around so she's staring down at me, and I hug her legs, slam my mask against her hard thighs, and, when my weight won't pull her down, I start the chainsaw for a few rounds, reach up, careful not to get her hair, and she falls into my arms.

Below us, out the window, the city's asleep. All the cars moving out there driven by sleeping people, just going through the motions.

I close my eyes too, so this can all be a dream.

So I won't have to know that the blouse she's wearing now, it's billowy, it's thin, it's not hers.

But it's all right, too.

I'm still here.

Because I'm a good person, I stretch the mask over her face, lower her down through the hole gently, and then slip down as well, my arms waving above me for a moment in exactly the way I don't need them to, ever.

Ten seconds later, I've got the little phone pressed hard into the side of my head.

Mary pretends to be asleep, but I know better.

What I should do is say I'll trade her. I'll magically get her daughter back to her if she can just wear that pretty blouse over, say.

What I shouldn't say is anything that lets her know that the mannequin suicide got to me. Anything that lets slip that I know what it means: she can get in downstairs without my knowing, and she can get in upstairs too. And Singer's goons have already been in the lefthand apartment, surprise surprise.

What's left?

She just wanted me to think the psychological campaign was over.

"What?" she says, her voice creaky with fake sleep. It reminds me.

"Hold on," I say back, and hang up neatly, dig the crinkly plastic out of the trash, wrap it around the phone. Then, instead of clay, I stuff my mouth with two heaping fingerfuls of butter, take a deep lungful of that cool white air in the refrigerator.

Okay.

I scroll down to her other number, the home-one, I think.

It rings and rings and rings.

I call her cell back.

"You're not at your place," I tell her.

"That's what it's like on the outside," she says, sitting up in bed, I think. Whatever bed. "You'd know that if, you know. Don't want to say anything to incriminate you."

"This isn't even me."

"Well then, yeah. One of the perks of not being in . . . let's just call it jail, okay? One of the perks, it's going wherever you want, at any time of day or night. You should try it sometime."

"Overrated. Been there, anyway."

"When?"

"Yeah. That's why I called. To answer your questions."

"Then why?"

"You're in your car," I say, going to the window.

There is one down there, parking lights on.

It begins to creep forward.

"Watch out for that bottle," I tell her.

The car doesn't stop.

Or, she knows that it's not supposed to stop, if it's going to keep not being her.

You can't put anything past her. This I know.

I rip the curtain shut, lean over the kitchen counter. Change ears, rubbing my sweaty hand over the prickle of my scalp.

"You're up late," she says then. "Guilty conscience?"

"Maybe I don't sleep."

"Eww, yeah. Scary. Good."

I don't dignify this.

I say, "You're in better shape than I thought. Unless the elevator's faster at night."

Now the quiet's all on her end.

"Been training," she finally says. "Why are you really calling, though? It's late."

I huff air out my nose at this.

Like I'm not her night, her day.

"Tell me more about him," I say. "You know."

It was what got her ramped up last time.

"Jack," she says.

"Yeah?" I say back, my voice too close to my real one for a moment. I cough it away, grind my throat down.

"Not you," she says, finally following. "Him. The real one."

What I almost slip and say back is *Riley*, pure ambush. But I bite my tongue. Hard.

Later. Save it.

"You would have liked him," she says, her voice not cracking at all this time. "Really, he used to say that between cops and killers, there was just a switch that gets flipped."

"I wouldn't go that far."

"Don't worry, I'm not saying you're either of those. You're special, aren't you?"

I thin my lips. Wish she was right here with me.

She knows it, laughs through her teeth.

"I did it earlier," she says then, *her* ambush. "Got you back for what you did."

"What I did to Dear Detective Jack."

"To my husband, yes. It's not enough, but it'll do, I think." She pauses, liking the way *husband* felt in her mouth, I think. "What's the worst thing you can imagine happening to you?" she asks then. "Pretend we're playing a game here. Truth or dare. Bottle's at you."

"Dare."

"Then I dare you to tell me what's the worst you can imagine happening to you."

"And what if I don't?"

"It'll happen anyway," she says. "It's already happening, really. Maybe we should cut this short. You might want to tidy up."

I breathe in, breathe out.

A line of sea foam, whispering towards me.

Something dark out there in the water, its back glistening for a moment in the moonlight.

Shit.

"It's not dying," she says for me then. "I know tough guys like you aren't scared of that. It's—"

"Nothing," I say. "The worst that can happen to me, I'd love it."

"What if you had to pay for something you didn't do? Would there be any pride in that, you think?"

I stare into the countertop, drool a thin line of butter out. Finally get it.

She's setting me up.

Not calling in the fuzz to come collect their next big news item, but—

I can't trace it out, though. There's nothing to trace.

"You were telling me about Jack, I think," I say.

"You don't have to do that to your voice."

"Got a bone in my throat."

She almost laughs at this, I think.

Whatever it was that got her to break down earlier, give up the nurse act, leave a voice mail of just breathing, she's over it. Got her nerve back. And then some.

What could she do to me that wouldn't involve the law?

"Jack," she starts off then. "He had a sick humor too. Most cops do. Even saved pictures of crime scenes, you know they did that?"

Yes. No.

"And here's something. I don't care what kind of childhood you had to make you what you are. He had worse."

"I'm jealous," I say.

"But you don't even know why, do you?"

I squint, blink fast, flipping pages back to what she could be talking about. The crime scene photos. "Same reason *I* might save them," I smile back. "Material for later."

"Why *you*."

"Doesn't matter."

"Of course not. Might make him human, right? Lot easier just being the woodchipper out behind the house. Just chop up whatever gets pushed your way."

"It's not like that."

"Don't lie to yourself," she hisses, losing it for a moment. "It's exactly like that."

I cover my mouth with my hand. Swallow.

"The reason he got pushed your way," she says, "it was because your boss thought he was turning his girlfriend into an informant. He thought Jack was telling her all about him. Trying to turn her against him."

This is good.

I wish I'd had it earlier, but it's good.

To Singer, if I'd known then: So you loved your little yoga princess so much that you've already got another lined up to take her place? What was that, *sir*?

Ha.

"It wasn't Jack's fault she killed herself like that, though," Mary says. "If that's even what happened, I mean."

I stop with the smiling. Run the dates.

Riley. She's been with me now for two years.

And I've been here for three.

And Jack—it's stupid.

Probably what happened was he was trying to flip the new Belinda, Singer's replacement blonde, and she freaked, swallowed all her meds, end of story.

Unless Singer left a year between daddy and daughter for

some reason. Unless he popped Detective Jack on the street one day himself, plenty of witnesses so it'd be sure to be legend, then, just as the pension checks were starting to stack up in Riley's college account, he took her away as well. Told her what everybody'd been saying at the funeral was wrong. That he knew where her daddy was, that her daddy gave him this badge so she'd know it was true.

Meaning that, if it *was* Belinda Dead Detective Jack had been trying to flip, then she didn't kill herself. Not exactly. Unless walking into my line of sight can count for suicide.

Which, yeah.

But the suicide Mary's talking about.

Maybe that's just what Singer told around town.

Otherwise he'd look weak, vulnerable.

Better to let her die a hero, let her choose death rather than betrayal, and then punish the cop who put her into that position. And his daughter as well, so the rest of the force would know to stay away. So everybody would know that this guy, he'll go after family too. And years later.

Look what he did to me, I mean.

Dispose of the evidence.

The fuck.

Not that I wouldn't appreciate the stupidity of it all either, if it really went down this way. The stupidity of Mary not being after me for her daughter, in a dark room next door, but for her husband, who I never even touched, or saw. But she's right, by taking Belinda into that storage room that day, I did kill him all the same. So she should be after me after all.

It's like it was meant to be, really, me and her.

Clockwork. Fate. Loaded dice.

Only, what if she knows all this somehow. Is leading me to think it, because it's more real coming from me?

One thing you have to learn to watch out for, it's when you notice that all the bricks you've got lined up around you, they're too even, too easy to count.

What that tends to mean is that you put them there yourself. And that they can all come falling down on you at any moment.

So I go with the next blonde instead. The unpoetic version. The one where daddy and daughter both got it during the same ice cream trip, only daddy went down hard, in the street, a very public hit, and then had to watch—and this I believe—his daughter be carried off into the night, her reaching back for him, him reaching ahead to her, fifty yards between their hands already.

That's more like it.

"Riley," I cut in then, right through whatever line of bullshit Mary's trying to feed me.

Silence. Nothing. All the sound in the world sucked back into one magic little phone.

"What did you say?" she asks, something shrieky and perfect in her voice. It makes my naked scalp crawl.

I smile one side of my mouth, can't help it.

"Her name is Riley," I say, then hang up before she can ask if she heard right.

Was, or is?

Yeah. Exactly.

Instead of carrying the mannequin back down to her upside-down post, I nail a cabinet hinge sideways over the corner of the trap door, smooth the carpet back down over it.

Downstairs doesn't exist for me anymore.

I'm sorry to the others down there, but—but it's like when you find a baby bird on the sidewalk, and try to cradle it back up to the nest. When Momma Bird floats home, she takes one sniff and her eyes go dull with disappointment. If she had lips, she'd purse them in right then, just keep to herself for a bit.

What I'm saying's that downstairs apartment, and the one under it, they don't smell right anymore. Probably won't for years.

And upstairs. Upstairs, I don't know.

For the time being, I take the headboard apart, cut it, nail it over the hole then nail the closet door shut too, only hitting each nail five times, even if it's not all the way in.

Like I need any of the clothes in there. Nothing I can't write on the list in the lefthand apartment anyway.

Was it like walking through Heaven though, being up there?

I can't tell yet.

Just like this place, my place, but paler. Less there. And empty, the waiting kind of empty, not the everybody's dead and gone kind.

It didn't even care, either, me cutting on the kitchen cabinet. If it could have, it would have even leaned into it, I think, or at least stretched the other way from the chainsaw, to tighten the wood on top, make it easier to get through.

And—shit.

The refrigerator door. It's fucking open.

The light'll burn through the linoleum in the kitchen first, and then'll be a dim glow in my ceiling, tapered like a coffin.

Not what you want to see at three in the morning.

Step into the light, Billy. We're all nice up here.

Yeah. Never heard that one before.

I push through the door to the lefthand apartment, write it on the list, for somebody to turn that damn light off. But then I erase it with the side of my fist. The less people know about it, the better.

It must have been a rush for her, though. Dashboard Mary. To be up there, walking through that pale reflection of here. Was it like she'd been picturing for so long? Did she put her fingertips to the walls and keep them there, sure she could hear the echoes of saws, of promises, of voices raised high and then cut off all at once, or was it all just practice for her, a walk-through, the camera in her head snapping, snapping?

I've got to remember that too, though, that she knows the floor plan now. That if she runs, it'll be with direction, not just wild, anywhere.

And—and why even hang a body up there in the window? That's the real question.

She doesn't *want* the cops here, right? Has bigger plans for me, I'm so scared, blah blah blah.

Too, how would she have known which mannequin to nab?

For a bad moment, a possibility I have to shy away from physically, I try to put together what I know for sure of her.

All it comes down to is a name on a phone. A woman walking away, across the street. Hands on a Girl Scout's shoulders.

Conversations that I can't start thinking I was having with myself.

A series of snapshots that I couldn't have dug from a dead detective's pockets, cut all the faces from, so I could be him.

No.

A Girl Scout uniform folded into the oven.

Cookies I shouldn't have eaten.

A mannequin hung by the neck in the upstairs apartment.

I back my way out of the bedroom, apologize to the wet-dry vac for the hundredth time—manners, manners—shrug into the plastic sleeves. The gas mask, so I won't have to see my eyes, reflected in the black television screen.

Soon enough the sun comes for me.

Behind me on the counter, Kid Hoodie's muttering headlines.

I cry into the mask and the old man across the way can't tell. That I'm human, even.

Before the sun's even all the way gone, there's a noise at my door. A muffled knock.

Instead of turning to look, I watch the mannequin's face.

She's by the window opposite me. On watch.

"Nothing, right?" I say to her.

She doesn't bat an eyelid, doesn't flutter a dimple.

I lower my head to my chest, the tube from the gas mask scraping my bare chest, holding my face up.

And then I come up different.

My robots arms test their joints. My mechanical voice hums.

"Somebody order pizza?" I call out, just generally.

No answer.

I push up from the chair, turn around.

"Too late for the mail lady," I say, just loud enough.

The knock comes again, hard enough that the whole door shakes in its frame. Three knocks, the first set not even died away proper yet.

"Couldn't be flowers," I say, "nobody sends me flowers anymore," and have my hand cupped to take the brass knob when—

Something's wrong.

I should have wired a Christmas bulb to the knob, so that if anybody's ever juicing it from the other side, I'll get an indicator light.

That doesn't help me now, though.

And anyway, don't be stupid: it would ground itself out whenever the door closed.

What, then?

"Who is it?" I singsong. Just another guy. Anybody.

In the hall somebody laughs. It lasts about as long as a cough.

Not Mary.

I cock my head, angle my face over to the closet for the little hatchet, buried again in the dusty bag, and, just on instinct, I angle my side in, for the shotgun blast I know's coming. That's been coming for years now.

Instead, I catch fire.

It starts at my foot.

The ankle rig, shit.

I never—

And then it's dialed all the way in, redlined, the little battery going for broke.

I look down in wonder, see the smoke wisping up along my shin, but after all these years it's barely enough to even curl the sole of my foot up from the floor.

And then it's dead, spent.

Too late, I realize I should have pushed something over. Something loud enough for the clunk of a falling body to make it through the floor, out into the hall.

This ankle rig I thought I knew six ways from Sunday, though, it's too interesting. I lift my foot up, suddenly lonely for the green light, and to keep my balance I go ahead and close my hand around the knob.

It's like reaching into boiling water.

It *is* getting juiced from the other side. Grounding out like I knew, but passing all that current, it's hot work.

I snap my hand back up to my face, like seeing it's going to make it better, and before I can even move, the sharp point of a fireman's axe thunks through the wood, stops a bare inch from my right eye.

And all I can do is watch.

"Again," somebody male out there says, and now the door's falling in on me. I try to push it off, but.

Singer's two thugs, the Hot Iron Boys, Prod 1 and Prod 2, they've each got a thick leg cocked up on it. One of them whipping his hand, the one he must have put on the knob. He's not looking away from me for an instant.

"You are a freak, aren't you?" he says.

The mask, the sleeves. No shirt. Stubble head.

"Let's find out," I say to him, and draw my lips away from my teeth, and am about to go down to hell and take two with me, thank you, when Singer steps into my apartment, a garage door looking remote in his hand, and it's like that first time he saw me, the way he looks down. Like I'm this thing that was supposed to have been poisoned out long ago. But here I am, still wriggling on his floor.

"Billy," he says, more identification than anything like a hello, then skirts the laid-down door, tilts his head behind him.

Prod 2 understands, peels the door up off me. Stands it back up where it goes, more or less.

When the slash from the axe is still there he grunts, lays the door halfway back down.

Prod 1 takes something from the inside pocket of his jacket.

A bumper sticker I can't read.

He scrapes the backing off with his teeth, presses it over the hole.

"Good as new," Singer says, his back to me so he can take the place in. "Oh, yeah," he shrugs to the Hot Iron Boys. As if in apology.

They smile, are just remembering too.

Such a fucking act.

Prod 1 balances the door open a second time, watches me stand, frisking me with his eyes. But then all his senses are with Prod 2.

From down toward the elevator there's the sound of feet slapping carpet. Slippers probably.

Prod 1 looks back to Singer for confirmation.

"Her?" Singer says, and when the answer's no he flourishes his hand up, is being extravagant today.

Prod 2 steps back, out of the doorway, and in the same motion deholsters a bull-barreled little pistol. Through the frame of the door all I can see's his long arm, the gun pointing like a finger, textbook form. And then it poofs, hardly even recoils.

Prod 1 leans on the doorframe, looks out. Nods appreciation.

Ten seconds later he walks back in with a body over his shoulder. He unloads it like a sack of feed. Chinese man, coffee on the front of his shirt, blood on the back.

"Cute," I say.

Prod 1 cuts a smile at me, winks like we're best friends here. Or like he's an uncle, about to rape me in the toy room while everybody else is eating turkey.

Then Prod 2 fills the doorway for a moment.

From his wide shape, a figure steps forward. A woman.

Clacky heels, black hair, milk-white skin.

She slashes her eyes over at me and never breaks stride.

Dashboard Mary.

Hello.

Singer's in the dining room, studying the wall between it and the lefthand apartment.

"You wrote something on the board the other day," he says, never once looking my way.

"Cookies," Prod 1 fills in.

"Thin mints," Prod 2 adds.

And now Singer turns to look at me, his face tilted so one eye's higher than the other, his eyebrow raised up into a question.

"I think it's time we had a talk," he says, and sits down at the table. Kid Hoodie's seat. Lot of cereal eating there.

Inside joke, I say in my head, to explain the smile nobody can see behind my mask.

The Hot Iron Boys set me up in my usual chair. Dashboard Mary standing over at my window. Studying the street. Not once has she looked at the mannequin in her billowy blouse.

Singer raps his knuckles on the tabletop. To wake me, I think. Or, like a gavel. Like I should pay attention now.

In the living room, Mary laughs to herself about something.

I weave my heavy head side to side, finally settle on Singer.

"Billy, Billy, Billy," he says.

"Thought you forgot about me," I say.

"Never," he says, his hand open on the table now, fingers spread. "I don't want you to ever worry about that, okay? You and me, our souls are coiled together, the way I see it. Two sides of the same coin, as it were."

"Pretty thick coin," I tell him.

He nods, looks over to Dashboard Mary.

"I don't know what to think here," he says at last. "You know her, that one?"

I study her as well. Lick my top lip once, in the mask.

What she said on the phone last time plays again in my head: *your boss.*

I should have picked up on it then. That it's not just about me. Could be that's the only reason Singer's here. Because he was listening in, and I didn't deny what she said. Didn't correct her, explain how I was a solo act. Not taking orders from him, anyway.

You don't get to where he is without instilling that into the people who work for you, I mean. Instilling it deep.

"I know her story, yeah," I say. Shrugging like it's nothing new to me, all the pretty little widows this city has to cry for. All the widows I've made.

I smile then, on accident: I've done it to her twice, really. As far as she knows.

Could be a first, there.

I thought she was special.

"Want me to, you know," I offer, knocking on the table too, once, but sneaking four fingers down to complete it. Just not as loud.

"The mask," Singer says.

I just stare at him through the plastic eyes.

"Dispose of her, you mean?" he says, and the way he smiles, it makes me flash on last time. In the storage unit. Disposing

187

of the evidence. Not leaving that unit until I'd cleaned up after myself. Buried her inside me.

I throw up into the mask. It pukes from the tube, slides off my knee, into the carpet. Nobody says anything.

"Mommy Dearest?" he says, flipping his chin to the mannequin by the window.

"Toy," I tell him.

"Really?" Singer says, like he knows better but's going to play along here.

Maybe he's peeled back through my history somehow. I have to assume he has. That he stole a print, had it run, looked me up down and sideways.

It doesn't change anything.

Well.

Except that it wasn't Mary in the upstairs apartment. Just her shirt.

Who it was was Singer, fucking with me. Of course the door up there was locked. He had the key, the super, a locksmith with a gun to his head. Whatever he needed.

I swallow a little of the leftover puke.

"So'd you bring the cookies then?" I say, spreading my fingers out on the tabletop. "That's why this . . . this little visit? I say some magic word?"

Singer chuckles to himself about this, makes himself stop, then leans forward slow enough that I have to watch and, still going slow-ass slow, pulls me closer with the tube descending from the mask, so that my plastic eyes are right to his face.

The sudden, just-enough pressure on the back my head, it has a caliber, I know.

I don't jerk away.

"If you've laid one finger on her," Singer says, his eyes open all the way, then can't finish. Has to just push me away.

The gun behind me pushes into my head and then it's gone. But still there, I know.

I touch the divot where it was, look sideways into the living room, at Dashboard Mary. Then back to Singer.

"You don't know anything about her," he says. "Just what she's told you, right?"

I study her again.

"Mary," he calls out, raising his hand like summoning a waitress.

When she doesn't turn around, the silent little pistol hisses again. The mannequin face just to the right of Mary shatters, dusts the air.

Not bad.

I should have protected her better, not left her out like this, but still: nice shooting. A dead eye. Something to remember.

Mary turns around, her cheeks sucked in, eyes hot.

It's the only way I know she's not with him.

It means I have a chance here.

Not like I'm the first person to ever sit here and think that, though.

Prod 1 sits Mary down at the table with us. Prod 2 still behind me. He won't even have to aim. At least some of me'll mist onto Singer.

It's the only real consolation I've got right now.

Over by the front door, the Chinese guy exhales or something, slumps over sideways. Has been dead his whole life already, was just waiting for that fast little slug to make it official.

"Never getting that stain out," Prod 2 says, about the Chinese guy.

"Don't think it's the coffee he's worried about," Prod 1 says back.

"They have to be here?" I say to Singer.

He doesn't answer.

"Mary Nacero," he says, nodding across the table to Dashboard Mary then over to me, "William Colton Hughes. The very first."

This is funny to him.

Anybody else, and they'd already be dead. Maybe even him, if there wasn't a shooter behind me.

"We've met," Dashboard Mary says, trying to see me through the gas mask, I think. Trying to see me but pretending like it doesn't matter.

Singer's whole frame shakes. With a laugh, I think. But a sob can look the same way.

There's the gun at the back of my scalp again. Singer shakes his head no.

The instant the gun scrapes away from my scalp—with stubble, you can feel which direction it's going—I whip around, already moving to the side, and then have the gun palmed, am guiding it past me.

I pull Prod 1 right to my face, my gas mask hose dangling between us, one thumb at the hollow of his wrist, the other dug up under his arm, near the pit.

And the gun, the whispery little gun, it's directed right at Singer.

"Do it," I say to Prod 2, his hot shot already out, about to dig into my side.

The current'll hit me but it'll hit Prod 1 too. Enough for his trigger finger to jerk.

Prod 2 gets it, raises his hands, takes a step back.

I nod, not sure what to do next, just that it's going to be bloody and loud and all at once, but Prod 2 isn't done yet.

In one smooth movement, he has Mary under one arm, a push dagger up under her throat.

At first I think he's already done it, made her into his own personal meat puppet, but then it's just a short, wide blade. Not into the neck yet.

"Save me the effort," I say to him.

"She's a gift," Singer says, suddenly right in my ear, the barrel of the pistol surely in his stomach. "We found her in the stairway." He laughs about this. To himself. Leans back. "You look all over the city for somebody, and then there they are, right in your own house."

I'm staring at her now, Mary.

"All over the city," I say, trying not to let it be a question.

But Singer's not stupid.

He settles back into his chair, says it: "Can we continue now, Billy?"

I breathe in, breathe out.

It feels good, because it's from Belinda, the breathing. Something I took from *him*.

I push Prod 1 away hard enough that his lower back catches on the countertop.

Before he's even got his balance he's firing.

The first shot whips by the left side of my head, leaves a tunnel of sound there, and the other does what he meant: clips the cheekbone flare of the mask. Pulls my head that way, bloodying my nose.

I pull the mask the rest of the way off and slam it on the table. Daring him.

Singer shakes his head no, though.

"I have need of your . . . your particular *proclivities*," he says to me, tilting his head over at Mary.

I turn to her and—it's beautiful—she narrows her eyes a bit, like we're at a high school reunion or something, one that happens in the cereal aisle on a Wednesday morning, then her mouth moves over some word she can't quite make anymore. The second time she tries to say it, she can't help herself anymore either. She's screaming. Not your usual kind either, that wells up slow, builds itself into something louder, but the down-deep way you scream if you're a kid and your mom's locked you in the closet, told you maybe she's going to burn the house down now, or maybe it's just a candle in the kitchen this time. All depends if you told the truth or not.

And she doesn't stop either, Mary, has reserves most women'll never get to know, and then's pulling from even deeper than that.

Singer smiles.

Without having to be told, Prod 2, magician that he is, pulls a clear plastic produce bag from his sleeve, wraps it cleanly over her face and pulls on it with both hands.

"Guess you were right," he says across Mary, to Singer.

"Shut up," Singer hisses, or whispers, or says with his hand, I don't know.

They're all far away from me.

Mary. She's all I'm watching.

Every scream, her eyes are locked on me.

It's kind of perfect.

"Okay," Singer says then, and, instead of finishing it, Prod 2 slams her face forward, into the table. She comes up vacant, blood and snot in the plastic folds.

One of my robot arms is already under the table, its hand sly and familiar at my crotch.

Sometimes you just can't help it.

When I sneak a guilty look over to Singer, though, the look on his face keeps me with him.

"I really hope you're about to tell me the truth," he says, and my hand stops, my head cocks, and that's all I have time for.

Prod 1 steps forward, clocks me behind the ear with the butt of his pistol.

When I can see again, it's through plastic. The same bag they used on Mary. Her snot and blood a distinct taste on my lips. My nose bleeding again.

"This is for your own good," Singer's saying.

We're in the living room. Mary's slumped beside me, still not with it.

"And, just so you know," Singer says, one of the Prods buzzing a hot shot into my chest.

My body arches away from the couch so I'm standing on my heels and the back of my head.

And then it's over.

Singer raises a green and white box up before me, tilts it from side to side.

Thin mints.

Behind him, all around us, the apartment's turned upside down. He's been looking for something. They've been looking for something.

That he's asking now, though, it means they didn't find it.

What?

"Girl Scout," I say, and Prod 2—I can see him now—starts to hit me again with the hot shot but Singer stops him.

"Girl Scout," he leads off, his eyes wet now.

"Girl Scouts sell those," I say. "Good, good."

He turns, stands, his hands pulling his hair.

He flings the thin mints box across the room. The cookies scatter. Probably make the air over there taste sweet for a few breaths.

Then he lowers himself before me, is sitting on the heels of his loafers now, his hands at his chin like he's praying here.

"I need you to tell me something, Billy," he says. "Just one thing. One, real thing."

I look to Prod 2, still too close.

"What?" I say.

"Did any girls ever try to sell you any cookies?"

More than anything, what he wants me to say here is no.

I'm not stupid.

I shake my head like this question is an insult, look to Prod 2 again.

He doesn't hit me.

"You know I don't eat that shit," I add.

Singer nods, keeps nodding. Already knew that.

"But you wrote it," he says. Like he's arguing my case now. To himself.

"The package they came in," I say. "That's what I wanted. Special delivery. YG, y'know? That a problem now, what?"

Singer squeezes his eyes shut. Hates to hear this but knows it's true too. That it fits.

Then he shakes his head, even more lost.

"She didn't come here," he says to himself then. In thanks, I think.

"I apologize for, for all this," he says, sweeping his hand around, and just when I'm starting to nod with him, Prod 1 takes both sides of my face bag, pulls it tight.

Singer turns, watches me fight it, then is on my lap all at once, his knee in my gut, his hands keeping mine from clawing through the plastic.

"*Did Alissa ever come here?*" he screams right into my mouth, his voice all shrieky and wrong, and I go slack.

Not Megan, but Alissa.

And then I understand.

How Dashboard Mary was setting me up.

Prod 2 hits me with his hot shot again but it's nothing, is happening to somebody else already.

I haven't breathed now in I don't know how long. Flashbulbs fizzing in my head, slower and quieter, quieter and slower, farther and farther apart, a universe dying.

But I understand. Could have loved her, I think, Dashboard Mary. Maybe even do.

What she did, how she paid Singer back for taking her husband, for taking her daughter, for feeding them to me, was to lure his own daughter down that same hall.

Except.

Except then she lost the nerve to go through with it.

That was what happened, what shook her.

She looked down my hallway and saw a girl about ten about to step in, and flashed on Riley doing the same thing.

And she was a mother, after all. She *is* a mother.

She couldn't let it happen, so came down, saved the little girl from the bad man. Her voice not even shaking.

But then. But *now*. Now she had this girl, this evil crime boss man's *daughter*, right?

Stop sleeping at home. Keep moving. Cell phone only.

There wouldn't be anywhere to run, though.

So.

So then you hide in the last place he'd ever look for you.

The stairway of the building you hate most in the world. The Chessire Arms. So close to the devil that he can't see you.

But he does.

And seeing you here, it confirms his worst suspicions. And you don't tell him anything different, won't say anything. So what he does then, he just takes you by the back of your arm, marches you upstairs. And the reason you go, the reason you go, it's because already in that upstairs apartment, because you gave it to him, there's that Girl Scout uniform. That *evidence.* And you'll get to see that look on his face. That I'll get ventilated first is obvious. Spread all over the fucking wall.

After that, however it goes down is all right.

He'll have paid with his daughter, worth more to him than anything, and I'll have paid with my life.

For Jack, for Riley.

We'll have paid and it'll be over.

The only problem is that the whole thing, it's hinging on that Girl Scout uniform I'm not supposed to have. Not supposed to even know about.

I try not to smile, but can't help it.

Singer pulls himself off me, lets me rip the plastic down from my face.

When I can say it, I do: "She—she took your kid, right?"

He nods, once.

"That's why—why nobody's been to my door for so long now," I say, balling the plastic up. "You've been worried, distra—"

"You don't know what I've been," he says.

I shrug, toss the plastic at Prod 2's face. It hits him in the shoulder.

"She hasn't been here," I say, wiping my face with my arm but the wet-dry vac sleeve hurts my nose. I shake my arm, sling it off. The other too. "*Nobody* has, boss man. Been kind of lonely, actually. Ask him."

Kid Hoodie, untouched on the counter.

Singer sneers at him.

"Then what'd she do with her?" he says, quieter. Not a boss now but a father, a daddy.

I just stare at him, like waiting for him to finish the question. Give me something to work with here.

He turns, seems to study the wall on the other side of the dining room table. Like he has no idea about the halfdoors in the closets, between apartments.

Just as well.

My life kind of depends on that.

I arch my back, trying to get it to pop.

There's two scorch marks on my stomach.

Later, I tell myself, rubbing my finger over their heat.

"Her name is Mary Nacero," he says, reciting. "Her husband, her husband, he. . . ."

"—was a police officer," I fill in.

"Detective," Singer corrects, finding his words at last but watching me too now. "That's what she does, mixes in truth with lies."

"What do you mean?"

"That's right, she wouldn't have told you. She's in grad school. Psychology."

I run my hand over the flare of her hip, pat her flank, give my attention back to Singer.

He shrugs. "What else do you need to know? She's not been very accepting of the hand life's dealt her."

"I did certain things with her daughter," I say.

"Don't—I don't want to know."

"You sent her to me."

"*Shut up already!*"

"Just saying. So she was smart?"

Singer nods, still not looking at me.

"While her husband was—while he was having discussions with my . . . with—"

"Belinda Two," I say. "The new yoga instructor."

He turns, evaluates me.

Not like I've gone too far, I don't think. But something.

It's not good.

"While her husband the detective was trying to turn her against me, I had some of her graduate work made available to me. One particular assignment held a certain . . . fascination, you could say. Behavioral Sciences. Design the perfect killer."

I smile too big. "She draw a picture of me?"

Singer doesn't acknowledge this.

"Her perfect killer was one that's been broken down, been made to face some big social taboo, so he just goes blank. Then you just come in through headphones, like it's their own voice talking to them, and tell them who they were before. Who they are now. Use the taboo to bridge the two, so it's the 'culmination and the continuation' is how she put it, I think."

"So she's saying everybody's a killer, right? They just need to let it out?"

Singer shrugs. "She got a D, had to redo it. So then, yes. She drew a picture of you, Billy."

I narrow my eyes, don't quite follow.

Singer opens his arms to take in the whole apartment. All of the Chessire Arms.

"She took a different angle in the rewrite. You find a real true mad-dog killer, then hand-deliver all his victims."

It's why she was screaming like that. She was in her own paper, now.

I nod, say, "It could work, yeah?"

Singer smiles with me, clamps his right hand onto my shoulder, and we study her together.

"Wake her," I say to Prod 2.

He looks to Singer for confirmation. "You heard him," Singer says without looking up.

Prod 2 hot shots her.

The couch goes dark with urine.

"It's gonna get worse," I say.

"My daughter's out there somewhere," Singer says back.

I nod, open my hand for Prod 2 to give me his blade.

He doesn't like it, but does, handle-first.

I snap it around easy, make like I'm going to push it back into him.

He flinches, the hot shot clattering against the coffee table.

I'm the only one smiling about it.

"Better get started then," I say, and kneel down over Dashboard Mary like I always knew I would. First I cut her jacket off, throw it behind me. Then, the way her shirt's hugging her.

I cut an up-and-down slit over each breast, then the bra too, so just her nipples stand through.

Prod 1 has to look away.

"Boss," Prod 2 says.

Singer shakes his head no, doesn't look away for an instant.

"Usually you have to work up to this," I say, "get her in the mood, but if you're on a schedule . . ."

"*Boss*," Prod 2 says again.

"This is where it all comes together for her," I say, running the flat of the blade around the nipple, waking it up, "both kinds of love, her husband, her daughter, it's all right here for her, right here."

Mary comes to, starts thrashing around, but I've got her arms pinned, my ass on her thighs. She's not going anywhere.

I make sure she sees my smile, too. Who's doing this to her. And liking it.

"You don't—he—he—" she starts, blubbering like they all do. Still calling me Jack, even. This isn't the phone anymore, though. This is real fucking life, baby.

I snap my hand behind me.

"Rob," Singer says to Prod 2, and then has to say it again.

Prod 2 gives me the plastic bag. I stuff it into her mouth, kiss her lips at the end, suck a little of the plastic my way.

Face to face, she goes calm.

Animals will do that too, past a certain point.

I push the bag in further, until she has to gag it back up a little. I want her here, not safe in her head.

And she's looking just dead into me, eyes all pooled up like she's sorry for me or something. It's her own narrow ass she should be concerned about here though.

Or. Not her *ass*, exactly.

"Take a picture," I tell her when she won't stop staring into me, then lean close, right to her ear, where Singer and Prod 2 can't hear. "Just shake your head no, no matter what," I tell her, and she goes stiff, my lips to the side of her face. It's almost like a kiss, but one she's taking *from* me.

I sit up, stare hard down into her to see if she understands.

She does. Thinks she does anyway. Can already see the two of us escaping this bad scene hand-in-hand like runaway newlyweds, her leading me through the streets because I can't stop squinting.

"Well then?" I say to her, for Singer, and she shakes her head back and forth no, tries to tongue the plastic out, is still saying something, *has* to say it: "ack, ack."

Jack.

"What?" Singer says, coming in close.

"She thinks he's going to come save her," I tell him, then more to her: "They all think that."

He nods, steps back, and I'm just leaning over her again to get down to business when a pistol's to the back of my head again. Singer on the other end this time.

I go still, don't get it.

"I'll do it," Singer's saying over my shoulder, to Dashboard Mary, like this isn't just exactly what she wants. "Just tell me where she is and it can all end right here. *Tell me!*"

She closes her eyes, is crying hard and fast now. Shaking her head back and forth. And then she does it, sucks the plastic in as deep as she can.

Her body starts to jerk.

"She's not going to say," I tell Singer.

The gun goes away.

Behind me, he's crying.

"Now?" I say, holding the knife to her breast, and when he doesn't say anything I finger the plastic from her mouth, sling it to the side. It sticks to the window, isn't sliding yet. The sun'll lens through it, if it stays up that long, yeah. Make a watery shadow on my thigh, maybe.

But that's later.

Now. Now I dig the stubby blade into the dark bumpy flesh around her nipple, saw a neat little circle until it comes away at the edges. At which point you have to twist it around a couple of times, finally wrench it away from all the ductwork.

If she was pregnant, you'd get a little blue line of milk there.

But that's all long behind this one.

When she faints away I slap her gently on the side of the face, say it while holding her bloody little pencil eraser up, to inspect: "Not all there anymore, are you?"

Prod 1 dry heaves, has to fall into the kitchen, the sink.

Amateur.

"What did you ask her the first time?" Singer says, standing now, I can tell. His voice booming down in a way I know I know.

"If she was going to tell us where your little girl was."

The *little girl* part is special for Singer.

It's enough. He steps forward, starts to beat into her face with the side of his pistol—he's crying the whole time, as bad as her—but her face gets sideways, so he's doing some real injury, catching her behind the ear one too many times.

She might still be breathing, but her walking days are over now, I'm pretty sure.

Luckily, I wasn't planning on her walking anywhere.

Finally Singer backs off, breathing hard, blood all up and down him, tears on his face, and then he sees me. Looks down to the bloodied pistol in his hand. Raises it like the most casual thing.

"You," he says, his lips contorting around all the things he wants to be saying here. He steps forward, so I have to step back, deep. "None of this," he says, "not if you—not if you hadn't."

"Belinda," I say, because I can see it on his face.

It shatters him, hearing her name.

"The mother," I add.

Alissa's.

Singer doesn't have to say yes. Just lifts the pistol up, steadier now. Right against my eyeball.

"Eat it," he whispers, flicking his eyes up to what I've got in my hand, "*dispose of the evidence*, Billy," more shrill, and it's that part that makes me start to retch a little.

I shake my head no, try to push away, but he follows.

"It's her connection," he's saying, "*bite through it*," and I wish so bad I still had the robot arms. Or that the wet-dry vac did. That it would come down the hall on its casters, the arms flailing above. To save me.

At least the mannequin's blind now, doesn't have to see this.

There's always something to be thankful for, if you look long enough.

I shake my head no, laugh a fake little laugh at this, my eyes full of tears, but do it somehow when he thumbs the ridged little hammer back. Lower the nipple to my mouth like a warm pepperoni. Close my lips over it, my throat already backing away, deeper into my head.

"All the way down," Singer says.

In the kitchen, Prod 1 is still puking. It doesn't help.

I chew and grin, the flesh elastic, a kind of elastic I remember from the storage unit, and I throw up into my mouth but Singer clamps his hand over my lips, doesn't let any out. "*Swallow*," he says, and I do. I do I do I do. Have to hold my throat closed with my hand, but I do.

Then he steps back.

Looks down to Dashboard Mary for a long time. Shakes his head at this, all of it. The waste.

"I was going to tell her where her—tell her what happened to her daughter," he says at last, sick with himself. "In trade." Then he shrugs, hooks the back of a knuckle under her jaw, flops her head over. "Hear that?" he says down to her.

No.

"She's yours," he says to me, throwing the gun onto her stomach. It slaps, sticks.

Prod 2 collects it. Wipes it down some.

"Sorry," Prod 2 says to me, his voice just flat now. Checked out.

I don't say anything.

"Ready yet?" Singer says to Prod 1.

Prod 1 leans up from the sink, nods. Wipes his mouth on the back of his sleeve.

He's washed out, doesn't say anything.

Behind me Mary moans, writhes a little.

"Traffic'll pick back up," Singer says back to me, without looking. "Way up, don't worry."

I stand on sick legs, push off the back of the couch to walk them out. It's what good hosts do. Except.

Except then there's a sound behind me. A creaky, baby bird groan that's not Mary.

I turn.

It's Riley. In the Girl Scout uniform.

She's standing somehow, years after the last time she did. Standing and wasted, no sun, her lips all—

She's not looking at me, though.

"I thought—thought I heard her," she's saying, her voice just barely there.

Prod 1 looks around, sees her, sees the Girl Scout uniform, and his hand is a snake, darting into his jacket for his pistol, for me.

This is my house, though.

Without breaking stride I reach up onto the fan blade with the tell-tale black screw, the little .22 already angled right for my hand, and pop him twice in the face, fast.

Prod 2 gets it in the cheekbone, from the side.

Singer stops, dead men on either side of him. The door's already balanced in his hand.

"I trust you've got enough barrels for all this," he says. The Hot Shot Boys. Chinese Coffee Man. Dashboard Mary.

I nod, don't say anything. Know that I'll never see him again, after this.

He keeps his face down, thinking about his little girl maybe, then looks back up. Holds the door to the side, steps out into the bright world.

I walk over, wedge the door into place, slide the chain home.

Chinese Coffee Man slumps over a little more.

I shoot him in the sternum until the gun's empty, then I'm standing at the countertop.

"Family portrait," Kid Hoodie says, about Riley, who's nuzzling into what's left of Dashboard Mary, and what I can see as clear as anything is Mary, knocking on some Mrs. Pease's door in some town just outside the city. Standing beside Mary is a kid, a young girl she doesn't know what else to do with. What Mary's saying, too, admitting, crying probably but not for the reasons Mrs. Pease thinks, is that she knew Jason ten years ago. That—*Alissa*. That Jason never knew. And then she hands Alissa over, runs away before Mrs. Pease can say anything.

Or something weepy like that.

I rub the top of Kid Hoodie's hood, use him to help me step over Mary's jacket to the sink, to get the electricity out of my mouth.

But then I don't get a drink.

Something's spilling from Mary's right pocket.

I lift the jacket up with a fork, shake it.

Confetti. It flutters down.

I smile, confused. Can't help but follow it.

"Throw me a parade?" I say, and pinch some of it up.

It's not confetti, though. Just a pocketful of faces.

I tilt my head over, narrow my eyes at the rest of it. Some of it's fallen on the snapshots already on the floor.

I smile. Of course.

The faces, I slide them into the holes in the snapshots, and some of them, some of them fit so perfectly.

Except then I'm shaking inside, some flap behind my nose forgetting how to open, that it's supposed to open so that the rest of me can keep living.

206

The face, the guy she cut out of the pictures, it's me. The guy I couldn't see, that she wouldn't let me see because I didn't deserve to.

The real reason she was screaming.

And then for an accidental moment I hear it, Singer's metronome voice filtering down into the blackest dark of the storage unit, my mouth full of pampered meat.

What he's saying is about how I got the scar on my hand. The story of it. Like he's remembering *for* me, telling me just because I forgot.

I hold my hand out before me, spread the fingers, study the burn marks so faint there, and then look behind me to Riley and Mary, on the couch together, and Kid Hoodie says it again, but different this time: *Family portrait.*

It's funny. I cry.

The snapshots and the pocketful of faces flutter down.

"Sweep them up later," I say out loud, my voice strange to me at first but then better. Back. I'm the worm. I live far above all this. I decide who lives, who doesn't.

I wait.

Days later, Mary installed in her room upstairs, Riley back in hers, me in my chair, Mary's face is on the screen, over the anchor's shoulder.

I'm greased up, the sun so nice.

What they're calling her is the missing detective's widow, missing herself.

Some of herself, anyway, I add.

I smile, go to another channel. Can hear the Deaf Vegetable Ghost next door. He doesn't know how loud he is.

I don't know.

I guess Singer thinks him not being able to hear, it'll give me what I need, or keep him safe, something.

What it's really doing, though, it's got me curious.

I have these two marbles in my cigar box by the microwave, see. Big ones.

I kind of want to hold him down on the floor one day, push those marbles in where his eyes used to be.

Mostly I just want to see if he'll still blink. If his eyelids won't get the message, will still be trying to keep this glass wet.

But not today.

Today it's warm, and right now in a smoky dim bar out there in the city, some girl with an unbreakable heart is pulling a slip of paper up from between her breasts, holding that address to her lips like a secret before passing it over.

In the yellowy light of the bar, then, maybe you try to read it already.

Everybody has a death wish, I mean.

The spider in me salutes the fly in you.

Tip of the hat: good day.

ACKNOWLEDGMENTS

Thanks to Brian Evenson's *Last Days*, for giving me nerve to finish this; to Nelson Taylor, for that cutting-the-grass-bit, which I just flat-out stole; to Gordon Lish, from whom I also unshamefacedly stole; to Kasey Ozymy and Anthony Putnicki, Kasey for documenting the love between a man and his appliances, Anthony for how a voice like this can sometimes work; to Gavin Pate, for a so-important first read, to Paul Tremblay for a second read, to Jonathan Heinen for a most-most important third read, to Christopher O'Riley and Christopher David Rosales for reads after that, and to Brenda Mills, for *trying* to try to read this one, anyway; to John Fowles and Vladimir Nabokov, for mapping out how novels like this can be done; to Jack Ketchum and Joe R. Lansdale, for taking it even further, and never once flinching; to Bret Easton Ellis, for showing that there could be smiles in there as well; to *White Hotel* and *The Life of Pi* and *Atonement*, for showing that made-up redemption can be the most real thing ever; to *Ubik* and *VALIS* and *A Scanner Darkly*, for showing one way to stumble in the direction of that redemption; to Neil Gaiman's *Coraline*, for cueing me into that PKD path, that once-upon-a-time Palahniuk shuffle; to Scott McCloud, for the ending; to Brian Aldiss, for a template;

to Carlton Mellick III and Jeremy Robert Johnson, for knowing what shouldn't really be done, then doing it anyway, and with a grin; to James Welch's *Winter in the Blood*, for showing a way a novel can be put together piece by little piece, so that it never comes apart; to Cormac McCarthy, for wending a tender route through all that, but leaving bloody footsteps, and to JDO, for following those footprints into the darkness. And, to an ex-stepdad, for taking a certain five-year-old to the caliche pit in Big Springs one unfine day, setting his beer down on the lip of a cliff and then stepping backwards into the open space just all at once, so that that screaming hysterical five-year-old would grow up one day with a distinct taste for this kind of stuff. Never mind that that stepdad was ten feet down on a little shelf of rock, holding on by his fingertips, laughing. Thank you. And thanks again and always times thirteen to my wife Nancy, who had no idea what I was writing this time down in the basement, but believed in me all the same. And would have even if she had known. Now it's out of my head for a while. All smiles.

ABOUT THE AUTHOR

Stephen Graham Jones is the *New York Times*-bestselling author of more than forty novels, collections, novellas, and comic books, including *The Only Good Indians* and the Indian Lake Trilogy. Jones received a National Endowment for the Arts fellowship and has won honors ranging from the Mark Twain American Voice in Literature Award to the Bram Stoker Award. Jones lives and teaches in Boulder, Colorado. Visit his website at stephengrahamjones.com.

STEPHEN GRAHAM JONES

FROM OPEN ROAD MEDIA

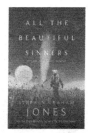

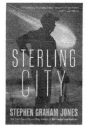

OPEN ROAD

INTEGRATED MEDIA